Siolution

Joe T. McCormack

Chronicles of the Realm, Book 3

First Edition: 2026
First Printing: 2026
Published by Imagicache, llc
Manufactured in the United States of America

siolution.work

ISBN-13: 979-8-9908219-6-5

PART IV

Chapter One

Within the main cavern of the Telluric Hollow Raudiim waved a multi-spectrum detector fitted with analog gauges, built by the hand of his Tart'aas ancestors, about the Aethereal Kinesis-Forge in order analyze its mechanical state and harmonic resonance. Of utmost concern was its crystalline integrity. While, even to the trained eye, the absence of visual breaks or cracks upon the surface or deeper within the forged crystal did not mean the powerful device was without blemish and would not shatter in a horrendous burst of energy during use. At this moment he was in search of micro-fractures, invisible to the eye, that concerned him. Those hidden slivers of structural impurity that could grow in a single moment and not only destroy the Forge but all those within the Telluric Hollow and even the cavern itself.

While the Forge continued its slow and dependable rotation before him, Raudiim braced the clipboard on his abdomen and forearm in order to jot down some of the readings with his other hand. He smiled briefly, comparing the results with those taken from before, relieved that the Forge's integrity was unchanged. Then he re-grasped the clipboard to focus on the two-foot-tall dodecagon shaped blue aventurine crystal columns, which circled the small pool at the base of the Forge, and moved the detector near them. After slowly walking around them while observing the detector, he recorded the readings. Like the Forge their readings, too, were consistent.

But just as he finished writing the faintest blue glimmer was caught from the corner of his eye, albeit for a split second. Immediately Raudiim frowned and looked between the columns and the detector, keen to notice anything out of the ordinary. For perhaps a minute nothing happened…no flash…no jolt of the gauges fashioned into the detector. Then another flash jumped out from all of the columns in unison, though more subdued than the first. Seeing no corresponding change with the detector, he dropped to his knees and held it over the columns just an inch from their flat tops in a bid to capture a reading from the sudden, mysterious, behavior. Raudiim remained completely motionless, as if frozen in time, only his eyes jumping between the crystal columns and the detector for another minute before they emitted another flash as equally faint as the second. Despite the physical manifestation, the detector revealed nothing…their structure and harmonic resonance was not compromised.

"What is going on here?" he whispered to himself, beginning to question whether the detector was functioning properly as he twisted it around with his hand. But, in fact, nothing was wrong with the detector.

Raudiim stood to face the Forge and again took readings with the detector. Still, it revealed nothing. Shaking his head he turned about and headed back to the hall chilled, not by the stable and cool temperature within the Hollow, but by the unexplainable and potentially dangerous behavior of the aventurine crystal.

Duly he noticed Phosx exit the hall and head toward the Hollow's exit, pre-occupied with examining the detector and glancing up occasionally to make sure he was walking in the right direction.

Once in the hall he proceeded directly to the operations hub where Nahts sat, dutifully watching the monitors around the electronic equipment and making subtle tuning adjustments from equipment sensors located throughout the Great Lakes. Nahts, while fifteen years younger than Raudiim, was just as dedicated to the Forge and Tart'aas technology as he was.

"Have you picked up any unusual energy surges in the area?" Raudiim asked after stopping next to him and scanning the monitors.

Nahts paused for a moment to recall all of the sensor telemetry and said, "No. Nothing out of the ordinary."

Raudiim tapped the detector a few times before setting it on a flat area of the narrow desk, "Well, this detector might need recalibration then."

Nahts glanced at the detector and then toward him saying, "That detector has over fifty hours of run time left before its next inspection. Are you sure?"

Raudiim sighed, still chilled by what he had seen. After a second he looked at Nahts, raising his hand as if to pinch something in the air, "I saw these brief flashes from the aventurine columns. But the detector did not sense anything."

"What?" Nahts squinted, picking up the detector to examine it more closely before he remembered, "Well it does not mean the detector is bad…though its lenses are tuned for the Forge itself. Maybe it was just light reflecting off one of the surfaces of the columns."

"No." Raudiim affirmed, vividly recalling the manifestation, "ALL of the columns flashed at the same time. From the inside."

Nahts placed the detector on the table and then pressed some keys on the control panel before him to play back the sensor readings, as they had been recorded, from the past hour across the monitors.

After examining the data along with Raudiim he recounted everything he knew about the Forge and said, "Nowhere in the mechanical drawings or design ledger does it say anything or caution about those crystals flashing."

Raudiim merely lifted his eyebrows and turned his eyes back toward Nahts, "Yes. So, what does it mean?"

"Honestly," Nahts let out as he turned toward Raudiim, "You must have seen something."

Raudiim placed his hands on his hips and growled defiantly, "I know what I saw, Nahts. And I was not imagining it."

Then, inexplicitly, the natural luminosity of the golden veins throughout the Hollow brightened.

Impulsively Raudiim reached out and grasped Nahts and mumbled, "You see that?"

After gaining some composure he said it again, this time in a stronger tone, "You see that? Nahts?!"

Nahts shrugged off Raudiim's hand and turned toward the monitors to see if anything changed, "Yes. But nothing is being detected."

"At last, you see. What does it mean?"

Nahts, fearing some sort of radiological event, loaded social media channels he kept watch over, onto one of the monitors, "For one, maybe you are not crazy. And two, some sort of nuclear event? That's the only thing I know of that would excite the natural decay rate of those veins."

When the veins' luminosity returned to their normal level Raudiim turned toward the monitor with the hyperactive media channels rapidly scrolling with comments.

After several moments Nahts revealed, "Good news is it is not nuclear. The bad news is it appears to be happening around the world?"

Raudiim tried his best to read the comments but could only catch a few of them at a time. "So, what is it? Fires? Fires could not do that."

"My god," Nahts gasped, "people are spontaneously combusting…collectively starting firestorms in dense cities."

Aghast, Raudiim drew back and boomed, "I'm telling the Elder!" Then, without pause, he ran off to find him and the others.

The highly irregular behavior of Raudiim aroused the curiosity of some of the people who had been eating nearby. So much so that they gradually got up and walked toward the operations hub.

Laser focused on learning more about what was happening, Nahts didn't notice them as he found the first live broadcast and message board from a lone streamer in the middle of Chicago, moved the video onto another monitor and enlarged it. Despite the gyrating footage showing structures of all sizes drowning in fire, the overbearing sounds of sirens, the gut-wrenching screams of horror and desperation and the faint labored pants of the unseen streamer, Nahts caught the glimpse of a young lady carrying a carefully wrapped baby and running ahead as if she knew the way out of the growing inferno. But just as she turned to run down an adjoining street she erupted and burst into flame, losing grasp of the burning baby and continuing to run, the streaks of her flaming silhouette dancing behind her until she barreled through the open doorway of a small convenience store. Almost instantly the hungry flames licking at product stands and mercilessly roaring into the old ceiling tiles overhead consumed the store and sprang forth to join the raging fires beyond.

"What the hell is that, Nahts?!" one of the people near him demanded.

"You see that?!" another in the small crowd burst out, "That person said it was a plague!"

"Nonsense." a lady in her forties challenged, "Plagues are biological, Tom. I would say this has been caused by some errant C.M.E. nobody knew about."

Tom looked at her for a split second before he pointed at the monitors, "That can't be. Somebody is out there streaming and look at all those chats. There's plenty of clear radio signal."

What nobody knew, save for Regnum, was that the raging fires induced by alien MSI technology had been part of the plan to exterminate billions of people and structures from the planet while they were clustered together, in advance of the approaching natural disasters which would wipe out and disperse the few survivors that might remain.

Just as Raudiim rounded the corner of the corridor that led to the spiral staircase, he spotted the Elder and four other giants, all donning their robes while they descended. "Elder! Cities are under attack by fire!"

"We know." the Elder acknowledged mightily as he rushed past followed closely by the others, "We shall stop this here but you must inform the other Hollows!"

"At once." Raudiim confirmed, following them until he reached the operations hub. There he paused briefly to watch them exit the hall before he settled at an adjoining control panel near Nahts to send out the emergency message and to monitor the Aethereal Kinesis-Forge.

"Raudiim." Nahts whispered, trying not be overheard by the small crowd near them, "If some of those messages are true, this really is happening around the world."

"The Elder knows." Raudiim said lowly, pausing momentarily to glance at the flurry of messages and streams from three different cities displayed on the monitors before he re-focused himself on the Forge, "Now, help me with the Forge. And take that shit off those monitors."

The four giants hastily assembled around the Aethereal Kinesis-Forge and grasped each other's shoulders with the two giants nearest the Elder raising their free arm in the direction of the Elder, the palms of their hands facing him. The Elder then raised his arm, palm outward, at the rotating Forge and attuned himself to it.

The invisible, slow, rhythmic waves that radiated from the Forge began flowing through him and the other giants, then upward and back down toward the Forge's flat top. As the tempo of the waves increased, water begin to rise out of the small pool and slowly envelope the surface of the Forge's massive inverted hexagonal pyramid, with each rhythmic wave producing a small ripple that moved upward in that thin sheet of water where a faint energetic hue separated the two and appeared to discolor the Forge. At the Forge's top, as water from the pool accumulated, it formed a pyramidion equal in its base to that of the Forge's but only one and a half feet in height, rotating in the opposite direction of the Forge. Each time the base of the two pyramids came into alignment as they rotated, a tremendous wave of energy pounded down into the pool, as if it were a gigantic smith's hammer striking an anvil. Yet, the three orbiting fluorite harmonization crystals held steady in their own rotation around the Forge and the surface of the pool below the Forge remained placid, less the rippling waves trailing the Forge's tip as it turned.

Once the Elder could feel they were harmonized with the Forge and the golden stripe on their robes began to radiate light from the waves of energy being captured and channeled as if each of them were giant capacitors, he raised his other hand toward the Forge and exhaled. Closing his eyes he projected himself, simultaneously, over Chicago, Portland, Los Angeles and all of the major population centers spread across the United States of America by feeling the kinetic and chaotic pockets of raging fire. Then, as he had done countless times before, he beckoned the oceans to join the clouds and visualized the air currents carrying the clouds to intensify and encircle the growing rings of fire. From an unseen force, the oceans became excited with parts bubbling and expelling tremendous volumes of mist high into the sky to be captured by the winds and toward the clouds. Within a few minutes the amassed clouds over those cities at higher elevation and with greater humidity darkened and blocked out light from the Sun and, amid mighty claps of thunder and lightning unlike any had heard or seen before, a deluge of rain not more than a few degrees above freezing, suddenly fell upon them.

The fires began to collapse in on themselves, as if in retreat, but refused to be quenched with enclaves of the fiery rings persisting. Reaching deeper within himself and, by extension, the other giants, the Elder channeled more into the Forge causing its rotational speed to increase. In turn the orbiting fluorite crystals increased their speed and the fury of the thunderstorms intensified.

But the Elder's endeavor over other cities, like Dallas and Phoenix with its desert climate and low elevation had less effect, having to overcome the earthly heat of the surrounding sands stretching hundreds of miles. Undeterred and resolute in saving as many as he possibly could, the Elder reached as far into himself as he could. In doing so a painful, piercing, sensation burst from his chest causing him to fall to his knees but his hands remained raised toward the Forge. The other giants stance began to wane as they, too, fought together to maintain their connection with the Elder and the Forge with the golden stripes of their robes radiating so much light that the entire cavern brightened as if the Sun itself had descended to be among them.

Furiously struggling to overcome the pain sprouting throughout his large body, the Elder poured the last of himself into the gargantuan energy flows and the cavern itself shook. Then, at last, the gathering thunderstorms coalesced and heaved, releasing themselves upon the remaining cities. But, despite his mastery, the Elder was only able to maintain elemental control for an agonizing fifty seconds before he collapsed, lifeless. Abruptly the discoloration of the pyramidion faded and along with it, so did the energy radiating from the stripes on the giants robes. The pyramidion's rotation slowed and the watery envelope covering it retreated and returned to the pool below.

Groggily, one of the giants knelt down and gently turned the Elder to see if he was okay. Unable to feel any life force after placing his hand upon the Elder's head and scanning over him, the giant looked up toward another and grieved, "The Elder is free. He is…free."

One of the giants gasped, as if he had been hit by a boulder and another retreated from the Forge while turning and moving toward the cavern's exit, "I will find Phosx!"

"Now this is a great child of yours." Phosx said telepathically to the black bear looking up at the giant. Phosx, holding the cub of eight months in one hand, gently poked at the playful creature and smiled.

After a moment, he lowered his hand to the earth and waited for the cub to return to its mother before he adjusted himself on the outcropping he was seated on and said, "She might grow to be bigger than you."

The black bear flattened one of her ears somewhat and narrowed her sight toward the giant, "Yes. I hope."

Hearing the sudden cracking of brush from far behind Phosx, the black bear instinctively moved near her cub to protect it and growled in his direction.

Phosx, puzzled by the black bear's sudden behavior, turned to look behind him before he, too, heard the noise. Standing, he realized the approaching form moving around the trees was that of a giant.

Within moments the giant, slightly out of breath, stopped before him, relieved, "Phosx! So glad I caught you!"

"Well, another minute or two and I would have been on my way to Dongting Hollow. But," Phosx confessed, pointing toward the cub, "I had to see the little one. Why are you in your robes out here anyway?"

The Telluric Hollow he was referring to was the one beneath Dongting Lake that locals have suspected, for thousands of years, to contain a cavern below the water.

The giant patted his robe lightly and exhaled, "Pursiellan has been freed. By tradition you are now the Elder of the robe."

Chapter Two

"General." Janus said flatly, waiting for the general to look in his direction before the AI motioned with its arm.

Annoyed by the interruption, the general begrudgingly lowered his arm causing the display of the Scalpel to switch off automatically, and turned toward the AI, "I see the fire rings, Janus. Do you have some actionable intel for me?"

Janus lowered its arm and tilted slightly, "I am still gathering telemetry and available data from all satellites, weather stations and observation systems around the planet."

General Lowinsky shook his head slightly, mystified by Janus' seemingly pointless interruption.

The AI analyzed the general's behavior, comparing it to all past interactions and concluded that the general was not associating the AI's beckoning motion with the need to communicate privately. Straightening itself, Janus pointed at the control panel and said, "May I speak to you for a moment?"

As the general walked toward Janus, Mac looked at Jacob and Lionak, "Can you believe those firestorms? I've never seen anything like it."

"Aye." Lionak nodded, turning to scan the Moon's bright surface, "I don't sense any magic in those fires. But it sure does not seem natural. Really strange for so many to have manifested at the same time."

"And so similar looking." Mac added.

Jacob squinted at them for a minute before he slowly turned toward the general and, in an agitated tone, asked, "General. Could DEW weapons do that?"

"Dew?" Lionak muttered, unfamiliar with the term.

The general knew Jacob was referring to the arsenal of Directed Energy Weapons the military had at its disposal but said nothing, stopping next to Janus and thinking of how to respond.

Janus glanced at the general before turning its head toward Jacob, "None of the orbital platforms have been activated and the ground units have not been deployed."

The general turned, momentarily, toward Jacob and admitted, "We don't have the capacity to hit that many targets in the U.S. at the same time. Or at that strength."

"I have confirmed information regarding the anomalous fire rings." Janus said openly, "The event has taken place in multiple countries, not just in the U.S."

"Well," the general shrugged, "definitely not our hardware then."

"No sir." Jacob agreed roughly, "But I had to ask."

"That's okay, Jacob." General Lowinsky said, turning back to Janus, "Good observation. My initial thought was a bit nuclear."

"So, what did you want?"

Janus lifted one of its hands toward the Scalpel and said, in a lowered tone, "If you look at your Scalpel, I'm afraid I have some bad news."

The general brought up the Scalpel, pressing a button to activate it and when it showed the scene of a massive crater and a range of military vehicles around it, he asked, "What am I looking at?"

Surprised, Janus said, "The destroyed remains of a vehicle in a crater."

General Lowinsky raised his eyebrows and looked up at the cyborg, almost forgetting that the AI was not trying to be sarcastic, "And?"

"And," Janus continued, "If you look closer at the vehicle, it is Jacob's."

"No." the general scowled as he stretched the video with the motion of his fingers, "Their wives and Zorin were in that truck."

"And the family canine."

"Damn. Did they survive?"

"Several medic and disaster recovery snap teams were able to extract everyone and are in-route to Fort Bloom by Blackhawk. Zorin appears to be stuck in dragon form and is being moved by ground with a HEMTT vehicle and escort." Janus said evenly. Janus was not aware that Chief Zorin's natural state was his dragon form.

"What is their condition?" the general asked, bracing for the worst news he could think of. It wouldn't be the first time for him.

Janus paused for a few seconds to scour the audio communication that had been, and was being actively recorded before saying, "Both Bev and Regan are critical but stable. None of the medical staff are familiar with dragon biology but the physical damage is extensive. They applied wound foam to seal as much as they could along with crudely linked elastic chest bandages…at this time Zorin is unresponsive but has a very faint double pulse. Or what they believe to be a pulse."

"I will remember that." Janus remarked to itself after a few seconds of silence while processing a different communication.

"What's that, Janus?"

"Oh. The recovery team noted that moving Zorin was like handling an armored sandbag the size of a small house."

"And the dog?" the general sighed, brushing off the comment and relieved that they were all alive at the moment.

"The canine is unconscious but appears to have less physical damage overall. More will be known after a veterinarian completes an examination."

"The children were not present?" the general asked, recalling Jacob's record.

"No." Janus replied and, after confirming personnel acquisition activity, reported, "Given geologic anomalies in the region, their family connection to Jacob and analysis of his parental mannerisms, a unit has been dispatched to retrieve and deliver them to Fort Bloom where they can be monitored, reunited and may also be of use with Bev's recovery thus ensuring Jacob's continued operational readiness."

"Good." General Lowinsky said gently before his voice hardened a bit, "Do you know what caused the accident?"

"Based on my analysis, it was from one of the Serpqhtaq Midcraft's weapons when they were engaged with two of your SSHC cruisers from the space fleet."

"Huh." the general grunted to himself, thinking about the probability of weapons fire from space striking a moving vehicle tens-of-thousands of miles away.

Just as the general gathered himself and turned back toward the others to deliver the unfortunate news, Janus announced, "A series of peculiar weather anomalies have just been detected. Weather patterns are shifting, gathering massive thunderstorms at the locations of the fire rings."

"What?!" General Lowinsky boomed out in surprise, switching the Scalpel's display back to one of the satellite views.

Jacob and the others gathered around him to see for themselves.

"I do not have any idea how that is possible at this time." Janus said as it parsed through the new data being gathered from hundreds of sources.

"Why burn and then drown everything?" Lionak questioned.

"Yeah, that makes no sense." Mac agreed.

"Analysis of event data preceding the fire rings has been completed." the AI volunteered, "Based on what I am currently observing, the two do not appear to be of the same origin."

Lifting his eyes from the Scalpel, Mac said, "What do you mean?"

"A collection of unregistered satellites materialized and beamed powerful electromagnetic waves down toward the Earth's surface shortly before the fire rings were detected." Janus reported, shifting its stance toward the others.

"Where are those satellites now?" the general inquired, eager to seize them at once.

"I am sending crash trajectories to you now. However, from all available data I have analyzed, the satellites disintegrated in the atmosphere."

Jacob darted his eyes to the cyborg and fumed, "Well, isn't that convenient. Is anyone else thinking what I am?"

"The aliens did it?" Mac suggested.

"You can bet your ass they did."

"I agree." Janus nodded, "All satellites must be registered before a launch and, even if a rogue state or corporation was able to get a payload into space without registration, one of the military's orbiting assets would have detected it even if it slipped past ground units and missile dome batteries."

Janus looked around the control room to hint at what it would say next, "Given that the unregistered satellites were not detected by the military's most advanced hardware, the dozens involved which were invisible just moments before the fire rings began appearing, and the coordination and targeting required means the probability that they are of Serpqhtaq design is exceptionally high."

"Or," the general shrugged, "there's another species out there we know nothing about."

"You are correct." Janus agreed, approximating a human grimace.

Jacob glared at the general, "I'm rolling the dice on the Serpqhtags."

Lionak felt the urge to correct Jacob's pronunciation but resisted it, electing instead to shake his head in agreement.

Mac frowned questioningly at Janus, "Why, after all this time, would they do that? Haven't they been here, like, for thousands of years?"

Janus turned its head toward the general and said, "General?"

"Go ahead, Janus." the general allowed. He was going to tell them soon anyway, and the information might dampen the impact of hearing about the accident.

"A Serpqhtaq colonization fleet is on its way here." Janus said plainly, "I've been able to confirm that with information stored in these systems, and will soon have a precise ingress vector of that fleet."

"Say what?!" Jacob blazed.

"How big is it?" Lionak asked with astonished eyes.

"Unknown." Janus replied, "Based on the definition of colonization versus invasion, I conclude it would not be that large."

"Shit." Mac whispered while he thought for a moment. Then, in a louder tone, he asked, "Why burn cities? Wouldn't you want to eliminate the military first?"

Mimicking human sternness and confidence, the AI crossed its arms over its chest and said, "If I had a relatively small but technologically superior force, I would first assess the military strength of my target and how it is sustained. In this case, your military is mediocre technologically, based on what has been deployed in-mass across the planet far outnumbering my military capacity in number. Extrapolating probabilities of multiple conflict outcomes, probes of weaknesses however insignificant they might be and given that I have a fixed volume of resources and limited strength, eventually your military would overcome mine."

"A protracted engagement is what you want to avoid." Jacob realized.

"Precisely." Janus grinned, "My fleet, so to speak, cannot be sustained indefinitely. Essentially you have infinite resupply capability and, as your military captures and reverse-engineers systems gained from contact, the technological state of your resupply evolves, reducing my technological superiority. Therefore, my first move must be to strangulate your military from its ability to resupply and evolve technologically."

"So, you destroy the populations that can be used to support resupply efforts along with manufacturing elements themselves." Jacob considered.

Janus looked between them all and uncrossed its arms, "Following that the board, as you would say, is mine. At times and places of my choosing I can launch direct engagements and lure the remains of your military into a plethora of traps they cannot escape. With sufficient tactical analysis of your military, it could even be manipulated to destroy what remnants of your species remain allowing me to preserve my finite resources for colonization and taking the entire planet without meaningful resistance."

"That's morbid." Mac groaned.

"Well," Janus pointed out, "it's the price of being technologically inferior and isolated on a single planet."

"It sounds hopeless." Lionak confessed.

"It is not." General Lowinsky rumbled defiantly.

Janus walked over to the edge of the control room to look at the Moon's surface and then into space, simulating what a human might do, and said, "The general is correct. He has already been working on making your species multiplanetary despite ingrained political chains and ancient, rigid control mechanisms designed to suppress your potential and keep you all imprisoned here. And I have the capability to infiltrate and understand the Serpqhtaq and their technology. Together we now have a plan to intercept that fleet before it gets here."

"Trust me." General Lowinsky voiced confidently as he strode over near Janus and turned toward them, "We will cripple and destroy that fleet before it gets here. Quickly and concisely."

Jacob narrowed his eyes at the general. In his experience he knew of no military campaign that was quick, let alone concise.

Mac scratched the side of his head for a second, looking at Jacob before turning in the direction of the general and assumed, "So you're going to fly all your spaceships to wherever that alien fleet is? Then pew. Pew-pew and its over?"

Jacob smirked at Mac's purposeful and somewhat sarcastic over-simplification.

The general's lips twisted for a moment as he mulled over the plans that had been made and were in motion before he said, "Not exactly like that. The fleet protecting Earth now will stay where they are. We have another nearing completion that will be sent instead."

"Then, as you so precisely articulated," the general jousted back while cupping his hands before separating them as if to mimic an explosion, "pew, pew. The aliens are dead."

"Hold on." Jacob said, both surprised and confused, "The AI said it just now discovered that a fleet was on its way here. Don't you need years to build all those ships, test run and fly them out? How long have you known they were coming?"

"When my command was established, decades ago, it was suspected we would face off against something back then. Granted, we didn't know exactly what at the time. Hence the space fleet was built. Better to have a sword and not need it, rather than need one and not have it. But you are right I, or more precisely, Janus here, did not know for sure until moments ago." the general shrugged.

Janus looked over to Jacob, "The ships that have been allocated are ones that are nearing build completion now. If the presence of the alien fleet had not been discovered, they would have replaced the fleet so the old ships could be retrofitted or decommissioned. The new spacecraft are technologically advanced versions of the existing space fleet…frigates, cruisers, battleships and destroyers."

The cyborg pointed upward briefly and admitted, "It is fortunate timing that the discovery was made now as the size of the space fleet will be double what it would have been otherwise. That lends to greater flexibility, more options, and a probabilistic outcome in our favor if the right moves are made."

"We'll be dispatching some of our most advanced weapon platforms to face-off against that colonization fleet. And we won't be geared for colonizing." the general reinforced.

Feeling a tingly sensation of strength and confidence ebb through him, Mac exclaimed, "Beating some alien ass and taking names!"

"Fuck taking names." Jacob retorted, weakly hitting Mac's chest with a balled fist.

Sensing the right moment had presented itself, the general took a few steps in their direction and said, "But before the ass-whipping starts, I have some important news I must tell you both."

"Oh?" Mac muttered curiously.

"Sure general." Jacob said, turning toward him, "What is it?"

General Lowinsky took off the Scalpel after depressing a small mechanical armature to switch it to always-on state, selected the video of the accident and handed it to Jacob.

"Your wives were involved in an accident." the General said slowly.

"What?!" Mac barked, completely unprepared and suddenly focused on Regan.

"Are you fucking kidding me." Jacob snapped, angling the Scalpel so the others could see the screen, "Are they okay?"

"What of Chief Zorin?" Lionak demanded out of concern for his friend.

Janus moved toward them and began to answer but the general got the jump on it, albeit by mere micro-seconds, "All of them are alive and in stable condition."

Janus peered at the general, curious as to why he did not also specify their physical state.

"The dragon…Zorin…is also alive but nobody knows how to treat him."

"Where are they being taken? We must go there immediately." Jacob said sternly though some of his words were broken by emotions of concern for his own wife, her physical injuries and how his children might react when he told them.

"Yes." Lionak joined, extending his hand and summoning the staff, "Let us depart. Now."

Janus reacted to Lionak's sudden brandishing of a staff it was in range of by taking a step back defensively and shifting focus to the wizard.

"It is going to take us some time to fly back to Fort Bloom where they are being taken care of." the general said calmly, feeling emotional darkness in the air and motioning toward Lionak to lower the staff.

"I will take us." Lionak grumbled, "A portal is much faster than your iron scabbard of a ship!"

The general gazed at Lionak and said, "Do you know where Fort Bloom is at?"

"Where we came from, is it not?"

"That was nowhere near Fort Bloom, my friend." the general revealed while he considered Lionak's statement. *'A portal would save a lot of flight time.'*

Disparaged, Lionak rested the end of his staff on the floor plating and looked toward the others for support.

"Still, you are right." the general piped up, "If you can portal us to where we launched from, I can get us on another SR-95 and fly to Fort Bloom. We could be on base within the hour."

"Let's do it." Jacob said to Lionak while handing the Scalpel to the general.

Smiling, Lionak turned, raised his staff and summoned a portal before them and was the first to step through it. Jacob and Mac followed closely behind.

"Will you join us?" the general asked, stopping in front of the portal.

"No general." Janus said while waving an open hand at the general and making its way to one of the control panels, "I have more work to do here. Besides, I am already at Fort Bloom."

The general exhaled to himself, still not accustomed to the fact that the AI had multiple avatars it occupied simultaneously, and sighed as he stepped through the portal, "Right."

Chapter Three

In the disarray caused by the sudden appearance of firestorms across the planet and subsequent destruction, an emergency session was called for the Council of the Thirteen at Crimson Portcullis. Due to logistical disruptions and some Representatives meeting their fiery end within those firestorms, only a few were able to attend.

"Is this all there is?" Frank complained, scanning all of the empty chairs around the ornately hand-crafted oval mahogany meeting table, "Three of us?"

Gregory, the Representative for Iter, stroked his short reddish-brown beard, meticulously trimmed to form a spear-point underneath his chin, and looked upon Michelle's chair hewn from extinct cedar trees and affixed with lambskin cushions. Then he focused on Frank and said, "Perhaps we should call off the emergency session. Even our Chair could not make it."

"Don't be ridiculous, Gregory." Frank countered as he sat in his assigned chair, secretly ecstatic that Michelle was not present, "We do not need the Chair's presence during an emergency."

"Maybe so," Karen said, the Representative for Serpens, strikingly attractive despite her long, crinkled ivory-white hair and years that surpassed Frank's, "but we have never had an emergency session without her. It would be highly irregular to start now."

Frank lowered his eyes toward the table and impatiently tapped upon it with his thumb. Undeterred, he pressed forward, "Given today's events I demand we…"

But before he could continue the only door into the room opened and a dark-clothed feminine form with red hair and golden-red eyes entered, followed by Ferina and trailed by a second dark-clothed male form, also with the same hair and eyes but bearing an unsightly scar stretching from above what remained of his ear that twisted down his neck toward the chest. After he closed the door, as one of the resurrected who fought alongside the Baron during their final battle, Ferina clasped her hands together in anticipation that she would need to introduce herself before anyone spoke.

"Who are you?" Frank thrusted toward her, annoyed by the disruption.

Ferina spotted Michelle's chair she had been told about and gracefully approached it and sat down. Surprised by how firm yet pleasant it felt, she grinned before meeting Frank's eyes and proclaimed, "I am Ferina, Michelle's regent."

"Regent?" Frank remarked, pointing toward Ferina while glancing at Karen, "Now that is irregular."

Karen rolled her eyes, "Come on Frank. Didn't you get the announcement? Michelle was summoned by her Mirror shortly before all this chaos."

Frank tapped the table a few times with his thumb, unwilling to admit he had not spent the time to stay abreast of such infrequent and typically fruitless messages.

Sensing the tension in the air and eager to find a way to establish her dominance over the others, as Michelle's rank imbued, Ferina shifted and said, "Can you believe all the destruction out there? And all those poor souls being burned alive? Simply gruesome."

"Indeed," Gregory noted, "I've never seen such sudden and complete destruction before."

"Look." Frank exhaled deeply, stopping to adjust one of the opulent rings on his fingers, "I'm both distraught and excited about those firestorms. Distraught because the event has thrown a monkey-wrench into the profits being generated from our flagship corporations out there. The widespread destruction has crippled logistics, economic output and labor. Ordinarily it's going to take months, perhaps years to recover from that. Which means, for the few competitors we still have to contend with, an opportunity for them to possibly gain market share and control over resources."

"You did not have a continuity plan created for this event?" Ferina made sure to point out in front of the others to add legitimacy to herself, "Do you have any plans?"

Frank briefly scanned the others, clearly unprepared for the incredibly relevant questions, "We do have plans. Umm, extinction level plans for events like a nuke exchange, glacial freeze, Carrington event, and flood because those had been measured already."

Ferina's mouth twitched, "Just not fires."

Frank focused on Ferina defensively and said, "With most of today's infrastructure built to shed fire until emergency services arrive, it was not considered necessary."

"I'd say your dependence on emergency services is a big shortfall. Especially since they clearly were overwhelmed…all over the planet."

Frank was not pleased by her assessment.

"Looks like a big blind spot to me, particularly in today's society where everything is so inter-dependent." Ferina proudly smirked, "You might want to give some consideration to worldwide fire in the future…and factor in the termite-like nature of fire both in and around our hubs of control. And, maybe, lose the infantile dependance on emergency services being there to save it."

"Anybody know who started all those fires? I'd like to shake their hand." Gregory asked, not particularly interested in hearing any more ranting.

"I'm afraid not, love." Karen answered with a concerned look on her face, "An operation of that scale we would have heard of or, Frank here, would have helped orchestrate to minimize disruption to our corporations under the umbrella of Fah."

Unlike their ancestors of cycles past, the Serpqhtaq no longer needed their unique traits, selected and bred over generations, ideally suited for suppressing the native species. With the Serpqhtaq empire having finally grown close enough to the Solar System with which to task a Serpqhtaq colonization fleet against, the Council would be left to suffer the same fate as the rest of humanity and be none the wiser.

"Yeah. The fact that we knew nothing and have lost an unknown amount of absolute control at this point is what worries me. Perfs must still be out there in force." Gregory admitted. He was referring to the word perfidy.

"I'm sure there still some perfs out there. Janus found quite a few usurpers but, with as well-prepared and organized as they are, I can't expect the artificial intelligence would catch everything. Speaking of that, Ferina, has Janus given you any updates? Michelle had helped to launch that system." Karen explained.

Flatfooted by the question regarding an artificial intelligence and her limited comprehension of the term and computers in general, Ferina leaned back and lied with a straight face, "Uh no. Janus is quite busy with what just happened. A lot of information to go through."

Ferina found it troubling that they had no apparent concern over the widespread human loss of their workers, whom were all trained and unified for the relentless pursuit of money above all else…the nectar of ego, corruption and even modern survival as enduring as the cold march of time itself. Grasping an armrest, and having pummeled upon Frank, she decided to confuse him further as to her intentions by shifting the conversation and pretending to share his sentiment and glean more about how he thought, "Please, Frank, continue with what you were saying. Why are you excited about the chaos?"

Frank, though surprised by Ferina's change toward him, grinned childishly, "That's the *Humanless Equation*. The chaos has eliminated so many, all at once. Meaning the amount of investment required to wipe out the rest will be minimal on our part."

Ferina stared blankly at Frank, thinking of how Mephistopha had been so suddenly diminished from the evaporation of much of the Arch-Demon's ethereal food source. Yet Frank, somehow, was so detached from his own species that he treated them as nothing more than wild beasts. Nothing more than a number on a spreadsheet.

Assuming her stare was an unformed question, Frank drug the small display tablet resting on the table toward him and picked it up to make some selections. Then he placed it on the table and pushed it toward her, and said with a smile of satisfaction, "You see that? The latest report we have suggests that four billion people have been roasted like pigs."

"And you really are not concerned about that?" Ferina asked weakly, skimming the report.

"I am from the standpoint that we are losing out on profits and some degree of control." Frank confessed while thinking of how to capitalize on the event, "That aside, everyone here knows we don't permit them to innovate for their prosperity. We strangulate them for our control. So, I'll come up with a scheme to take advantage of this control opportunity under, oh, the guise of helping humanity recover from tragedy and rebuilding lives by corralling them into free housing units we own where we can dictate costs of water, electricity and so on. The masses love being perceived as the center of attention. That there is some benevolent force out there like their parents that will coddle them. Protect them. Keep them safe."

"Aye." Gregory nodded, "They eat that shit up every time, and beg for more. Particularly the free part."

"And you, at least Michelle, knows this..." Frank frowned toward Ferina, "the ungrateful, ignorant masses have never deserved to live on our planet anyway. And up until recently, we've had no choice but to stay our hand and coddle them like children, dangling candy in one hand while slowly trapping them with the other. I think you'll agree that today's events are the sign that we can be more forthcoming with their erasure."

"So, just like that, you are ready to cut off the foundation that perpetuated and fed your control pyramid?" Ferina challenged softly.

Frank rested both hands on the edge of the table and prodded, "Are you talking about the pathetic S.P.P. declaration from a time when they could truly have been a threat?"

"S.P.P.?"

The S.P.P., though dated, has served as the tried-and-true template for their continuous accumulation of control and subjugation to the present day.

"What he is referring to is the *Cruenta porcorum decretum.*" Karen volunteered, recalling the ancient neo-latin writing tattooed into leathered human skin which had been meticulously treated so that it would endure longer than what was commonly seen with the skins of other mammals.

"Such a primitive and unimaginative document." Gregory winced, recalling his dread at being forced to learn and recite it many years ago, "And from an equally primitive and dead language. It is what we call the Stuck Pig Program. S.P.P."

"The bleeding pig decree has a certain ring to it, primitive or not, Gregory. Besides, in those primitive, simple times they were further from truths being revealed than most are today…so elaborate designs were not really needed." Karen sighed defensively, "But, for Ferina's sake let me explain. In a nutshell, it was drawn up centuries ago when a small band of rebellious millionaires and well-connected businessmen broke ranks from the aristocracy to gain independence and become competitors to the hegemonic domination of all life and resources that had once ruled across the continent. To prevent that from ever happening again, thereby guaranteeing total control over everything, like feudalism had once guaranteed, the secret decree was drawn up which has just two rules to follow."

"Let me guess," Ferina proposed, only aware of a single country in recent history that dared to stand alone, "You are referring to those that started the United States?"

Karen beamed her approval and said, "Someone who knows their history. Bravo my lady."

Ferina smiled warmly in return and asked, "So what are the two rules?"

After sweeping her hair back behind her shoulders, Karen took a moment to recall them and said, "The first rule is to inflict continuous corruption of the body, not only to weaken it but to weaken the clarity of mind. The second rule is to inflict continuous depravation of free thought and truth."

"Humm. I can guess about how to fulfill the first rule by poisoning." Ferina puzzled aloud, "But the second. How do you stop someone from thinking their own thoughts…and truth? Ignorance?"

"That is the single, most effective means." Frank confirmed before elaborating, "But, at that time, small printing presses had multiplied and spread beyond the Council's control so the written word could no longer be hidden or corrupted so easily by scribes copying and distributing texts. So, to counter the output of those presses, a shift was made to pollute all literature using our own to corrupt those who were not ignorant. By clouding the mind in such a way, those literate ones are deprived of free thought and truth and become literately ignorant by their own hand. They may inadvertently read truth that escaped our grasp but not know it to be so."

"Ergo, the weakened mind remains malleable to our dictates and oblivious to their demise." Frank expressed coldly, "We remain in control because we alone know what the truth really is."

At that moment Ferina realized that attempting to shift Frank's mindset through conversation and suggestion may not be possible. Still, she suggested, "Well there must be some out there worthy of being spared."

"Are you serious?" Frank grunted, leaning back in his chair and looking toward the others. Inwardly he wondered what mental game Ferina was playing to feign concern for ingrates since Michelle would never do such a thing unless there was something for her to gain.

Several moments passed before he continued with his justification, "Take the *Recalcitrant Report.* That has been used for centuries to measure workers and declines in productivity in proportion to self-appointed beliefs in entitlement and their individual importance which typically gain root based on changes in economic mobility across social classes. The ingrate marker tells us that when the masses reach a certain level of disillusion from fulfilling our interests and dictates alone that, for us to continue reaping gains from their blind sacrifices, we must shift and invest in another herd."

"You mean slave. Ignorant slave class to be more precise." Ferina blurted out impulsively.

"Yes, exactly." Frank confirmed, raising his eyebrows, "And while that herd collapses and loses the self-importance and belief that they matter and can shape destiny like we do, we reap profits atop the next and on and on until we circle back to that first herd, once again ignorant and pathetic to start the cycle over again. But honestly, things were so much easier for us when feudalism reigned and we could openly plunder the riches and abundance of the planet while being worshipped by them for doing so. We never had to disrupt or move anything and nobody stood in our way. Everything was stable and as it was meant to be."

Gregory hit the table with the palm of his hand a few times in agreement and gleefully admitted, "Ah those were the days! Imagine the completeness of life knowing everyone is fighting to do lip compressions on your ass in return for some trivial favor or trinket. I definitely slept better back then!"

Frank chuckled lightly in agreement.

Ferina, knowing that Mephistopha did not seek the extinction of the human race, and herself incapable of such extreme psychotic behavior declared, "Well, I will not support the summary sacrifice of humanity. They might have more wit than a tree and require us, on rare occasion, to think of new ways to chop them down, but they have amassed everything we have entirely at their own expense."

Frank gave her a disgusted look and said, "They should sacrifice everything for us. Pathetic ingrates anyway. We were chosen because we are special. We are of them but we are not in them!"

Feeling the rising tension in the room, Ferina's female compatriot stiffened her back in anticipation, and desire, to extinguish Frank and the other strangers, not for the discussion at hand, but for the pleasure and satisfaction of burying talons deep into their inferior flesh to silence them.

"You really think you are exempt from the Humanless Equation of yours?" Ferina hissed at him, nearly ready to lurch onto the table and kick his plump face.

Frank leaned against the armrest of his chair and glared between everyone seated at the table before exhaling slowly and thinking for a few moments and shifting himself against the other armrest. Then he confessed, "The Humanless Equation is not something us, the Council of the Thirteen, thought of unlike the S.P.P. It is our highest goal. It is our one opportunity to be seated among the Covenant themselves. Our masters. And, in the process, become immortal as they are and know the universe as they do."

"Faced with death, wouldn't you freely surrender what is not yours in exchange for life?" Gregory added, "It's not like you have to give up something you already own. You lose nothing. And, I suppose if you miss the ignorant herds that much, with the technology and knowledge you gain, in time you could bring some back as play-things."

Ferina's stomach churned with nauseous unease realizing how ill-prepared she was for this meeting. For exposing herself to those with absolutely no humanity and no capacity to see beyond themselves. Devoid of empathy to pluck upon, she accepted the fact she would be forced to use an entirely different means to seize control of the Council.

Regaining her composure and at the same time regretting she had come, Ferina finally said, "Maybe."

"See, I knew you would understand." Frank cheered.

Leaning forward, Karen suggested to Frank, "Go on Frank. Tell her what your plan is for all that new AI tech stuff you've been tinkering with that will give us absolute dominion over the entire Earth and completion of the Humanless Equation."

Frank blushed for a moment over the recognition of his newest schemes that, indeed, he did devote considerable focus, and said, "Ah yes, our own AI to compliment the surveillance capacity of the Mizuchi and Makara. Okay. Well. It was not all my idea so let me call in my guy that's been leading the tech work based on some objectives I gave him. He has been so eager to please and, I might add, well rewarded."

With that he pressed a button on the tablet and said, "Bring in Ralph for the briefing."

Moments later the door opened and a man, somewhat shorter than Ferina and dressed in gray slacks, a blue-striped plaid turtleneck shirt and matching gray overcoat entered while adjusting the large spectacles resting on the bridge of his nose. His receding hairline and peppered gray and black hair conveyed his advanced age while his timid behavior conveyed an aversion to social interaction.

"Ralph!" Frank announced to everyone, "Please. Be seated anywhere. And tell us what you have been working on for the Council and Fah."

After awkwardly sitting in a chair near Frank, Ralph nodded nervously towards everyone and said, "Thank you for the opportunity to talk about how technologies I've been overseeing will benefit the Council and, I hope, humanity."

With a glazed expression Frank winked at Karen and Gregory before he turned toward Ralph, "Please. Why don't you start with the AI data monoliths."

"Yes." Ralph responded, taking the tablet and loading the 3d model. Shortly after clicking the button to project it, a rotating holographic model of a skyscraper appeared at the table's center, suspended a few inches above its surface.

"As you can see, the AI data monoliths are skyscrapers. Using this one as an example, this skyscraper is being repurposed and retrofitted to house all of the hardware needed to support the storage of all data within a state or province…depending on which country it is established in." Ralph said plainly.

"Skyscraper? Why?" Gregory inquired.

Ralph began to speak but Frank raised his hand, knowing where Gregory was going and explained, "Price, for one. There's quite a lot of financially destressed lots out there that we can take advantage of. Two, like is true of all real estate, location. With them being in dense population centers, the speed of capturing and processing data from so many sources is almost instantaneous and the investment and maintenance costs remain low over time. Third, established power distribution and gigantic water pipeline networks are already in place that we can, for minimal cost, re-route or augment as needed. Forth, ready support from the city for power, water and most importantly, rapid response law enforcement to protect our monoliths. It is much easier to protect a square block with few entry points than perhaps ten or more acres of buildings at the outskirts of a city."

Gregory smirked at Frank, "You saw what just happened, didn't you? Densely populated cities were just burnt up."

"Keep in mind this was planned before the great cook-off." Frank pointed out, shrugging off his point, "Don't forget those structures have stringent building and fire protections built into them, so they will endure even if what's inside them burns up. Since we have to gut them anyway, I'd say what just happened is a net win. Please continue, Ralph."

"Yes." Ralph smiled, pointing at the hologram, "As you can see here, the skyscraper has elevator shafts that transverse its length. Since the skyscraper will not be facilitating the movement of people, those shafts are repurposed for power distribution and water pipes to feed a large water reservoir at the top to supply enough water to allow the hardware systems to be safely powered down in the event the main water supply is cut off. Otherwise, the reservoir functions to assist circulating incoming water with the benefit of additional pressure into the coolant systems to lower water temperature for distribution down into another shaft to cool the hardware on each floor with the most kinetic hardware located on the top floors and the least kinetic on the lower floors. Then, at the bottom, the heated water is piped out into the city's return system where, through transiting dozens of miles of buried pipeline and the process of thermal conductance, the water is cooled back down."

"Also," Ralph said, temporarily focusing on the tablet to illuminate the next part of the hologram, "The top floors have their windows replaced with reinforced plate to protect our most valuable hardware from adverse weather conditions while the lower floors have their windows replaced with vents, to pull cool air through those floors to offset heat that the water system may not be able to capture."

"And how are people that need to fix this hardware going to get around?" Karen asked.

"Every skyscraper has a staircase for people to use when elevators are not in service." Ralph pointed out, illuminating that part of the hologram.

"Are any of these monoliths in operation now?" Gregory asked, skeptical about overhauling a skyscraper as Ralph had described.

Ralph looked at Frank with a questioning expression and once Frank nodded, he revealed, "Yes. The pilot for the monolith program has been setup using a skyscraper in Norway, north of Oslo. This time of year, you have to admit the skyscraper looks like it is alive."

With that, he replaced the hologram with a 360-degree video view of the snow-blanketed skyscraper, surrounded by snowy terrain at early dawn, with the lower floors bellowing hot steam reaching up into the sky and above them shallow, melted snow streaks at various heights strikingly similar to inverted, long, pointed teeth revealing the silvery finish of the skyscraper's walls.

"And what is the price tag to get these monoliths built around the world?" Ferina probed, curiously attracted to the visual appearance of the skyscraper in contrast to its surroundings.

"About eleven trillion dollars." Frank sighed nonchalantly, "Peanuts compared to our reserve and well worth it to have embedded in every country."

Ferina gawked at Frank a little more openly than she would have liked, taken aback by the number he quoted.

"Any problems with it yet? Like water?" Karen asked, placing her forearms on the table. She had a suspicion, given all the talk of water usage and cooling, the pilot case might have been completed in a colder climate to gloss over such a problem.

Ralph shook his head, "Umm, no. None at the moment."

Karen squinted a bit and said, "Excellent. I would like to get the operations reports on that monolith."

Ralph briefly looked at Frank before responding, "I will do that at once."

After a few moments of silence, Frank spurred Ralph forward, "Great work with the data monolith, Ralph. Go ahead and tell us about the *AI Scribe*."

"Now that is a marvelous achievement for us all." Ralph beamed, barely able to contain his excitement, "Imagine having a tool at your side that helps when you need it, works indefinitely, never sleeps and can do just about anything you can imagine which requires computation. Analysis. Research. Really, just about anything that needs thought."

While Ferina, new to the subject stared intently at Ralph, both Karen and Gregory remained more passive having already been acclimatized to some interaction with the AI referred to as Janus.

In an attempt to get them more interested, Ralph decided to deviate a little from what he had prepared and said, "But you probably already knew that about AI. So, I'd like to tell you something about AI you probably have not heard before. One of many unique uses for it."

Frank looked at them and then to Ralph, interested in seeing where he was going.

Ralph inhaled and presented the photograph of a ghostly aberration and said, "The supernatural."

"Supernatural?" Gregory echoed. That would not have been his first choice.

"Yes! We know so little about the supernatural. Yet, for us to see it, like in this photo, means it exists. That it is energetic. Which means the energy can be analyzed and classified by AI way faster than a person."

"So, it can help us know everything about different phenomena?" Ferina volunteered, intrigued by the possibility of knowing the workings of the unknowable.

"But more than that." Ralph grinned toward Ferina, "Once AI has analyzed such things, AI could interact with those forces. Or, defend us from those things, like jinn or demons or ghosts at all hours of the day or night. Better yet, perform exorcisms and the like by using harmonic energy of some type. Can you imagine the possibilities with that alone?"

Karen and Gregory looked at each other, interested with the idea of communication, though Karen thought about the possibility of being able to push aside ritual entirely. Then Karen said, "So I could just call some force out there and talk, like we do with each other and a phone?"

Ralph shrugged, "I do not see why not. The sensory hardware would just need to be built for the AI to interface with. Maybe something similar to what you would do with an app on your phone interacting with a drone or remote camera."

"Okay." Frank interrupted, waving his hands in the air, "Enough wishy-washy talk. Let's get back to the scribe, please?"

Ralph cleared his throat and continued, "The AI Scribe. Think of it as the real-time arbiter of the data housed in each monolith. With access to all of that data, and cooperative task completion between monoliths for data one may not possess, the AI Scribe can really act to collect, analyze, research, compile, report and make decisions on any known topic. And do so for everyone, everywhere. There would be nothing that it would not know. It would enhance people, businesses and governments and they would be able to work much more efficiently. And, not forgetting your important work, it will allow the Council to do the needful things as well."

At that moment Ferina recognized that her control over the Council, if not achievable with intellectual jockeying and the bias of regent, might be achievable by using the AI Scribe's capabilities against the members themselves. She crossed her arms in contemplation and said, "Ralph, that was an excellent presentation. Thank you so much."

"Thanks. You are welcome." Ralph replied with a big smile, appreciative that at least Ferina shared his enthusiasm of the technology and how it might improve the human condition.

"I second that. Congratulations are in order." Frank grinned, rising from his chair to shake Ralph's much smaller hand, "Thank you for such a great presentation and I'll catch up with you later. For now, we must tackle the next item on our meeting agenda."

"Sure!" Ralph confirmed, nodding awkwardly towards them as he turned and exited the room.

After the door shut, Frank dropped his smile and sat down in his chair, leaning some of his weight onto the table's edge with his hands and peered intently at each of them. Then he exhaled and leaned back in his chair saying, "Okay. That's the nerdy tech stuff for my plan."

Gregory tugged on his beard. Then he said, "I get that having monoliths in every country will allow faster speeds and all that, but are so many actually needed?"

"Absolutely." Frank replied, "It ensures redundancy of our data monopoly and it ensures our broadest reach to the ingrates and competitors that are still around."

"I guess I am missing something here, Frank." Karen volunteered, "Let's say we have a monopoly on holding all data. Is your plan to just charge exorbitant fees to access or save data? I don't see that as a win for us long-term. To the contrary I think that would create more competitors for us and weaken control."

Frank grasped one hand with the other in front of his chest and revealed, "I hate to refer to it, again, but let's think back to just before the S.P.P. We lost absolute control over the ingrates because of low-cost advances that allowed those rebel-rousers to challenge what our scribes dutifully rewrote in our favor. And in greater volume."

"Sure. But over time we've bought out or had most of those distribution sources bankrupted." Karen pointed out.

"And, for a time, our near monopoly had served us well, allowing us to exert our control over all people and maneuver them and corporate competitors where we wanted them to go. Ultimately strengthening our position. But," Frank said, crossing his arms over his chest, "now we are back to the same position we were centuries ago where there are far more rebel-rousers, each a printing press so to speak, challenging us than what our managed distribution sources can overcome, despite broad corruption of social structures and prevailing literature. In this case, data."

"So…the AI Scribe?" Gregory said, not entirely able to grasp Frank's point, but suspicious it had a role

"That is our gatekeeper, like our scribes of old. In charge of orchestrating the data in real-time as it goes in or out of our monoliths, our scribes can revise or rewrite it as we desire and under a happy term like *smart clarity content.* Actually, faster than any rebel-rouser can create." Frank happily gloated, "So, no longer will we suffer from shutting down one of them only after their information had already been released. And we can dispense of all the agents we have to construct and maintain counter narratives. Which, I might add, will save us oodles of money."

"Then, what you are saying is that the AI Scribes will allow rebel-rousers to continue to challenge and distribute to their heart's desire but what is actually seen is what we want to be seen." Gregory surmised.

"Yes, and with the speed and intelligence built into them, they can even manipulate and fabricate live streams as they pass through our infrastructure, so even those exit with the message we want distributed. And what's even better is our AI Scribes become more powerful and all-encompassing the more they are used."

Karen grinned and said, "And we can even compromise our competitors through the data they get and they would be none-the-wiser. We really would have total control. That is genius."

"Right, we steer competitors into making devastating decisions. The rebel-rousers, sooner or later, will simply burn themselves out and evaporate once they realize that, no matter what they do, their insubordination to our order matters not and actually helps us." Frank confirmed as he grasped the ends of the armrests, "And our expense is nothing more than some of our guidance for the scribes. Just like the paradise we used to have."

"Even if they do not burn themselves out," Karen injected after whisking her hair back, "let's not forget that with our monopoly we can also impose randomized internet curfews that follow them around so they never know what device, when or for how long, they'll be able to connect."

"Indeed, that can be useful." Ferina admitted, "But I do not see how your scribes can materially affect the ingrates, as you call them, for more than a hit of internet."

"That is quite simple, actually." Frank said, pausing to consider what he said next, "Through our broad control of social structures and many corporations, we inject the scribes into every activity as fast as possible. So fast, in fact, nobody has the time or clarity of thought to challenge it. By sheer speed and totality, we wipe out human participation in all means of production thereby wiping out their independence, their source of income, their perceived purpose and devolving them into a permanent condition of lethargic ignorance, receptive to only what we want them to know through our scribes…where they are entirely dependent upon us for their very survival. Where each of them are tagged, tracked and ultimately terminated."

Karen moved, considering what she might add regarding production and income, the *Peon's Ploy*. It was a mechanism, integrated into all their corporations, for draining value from employees through the extraction of additional labor, given freely, without paying additional compensation for that labor by claiming to support their professional and personal development. The tactic leverages employee buy-in by having them specify: 1. choice of development they want, 2. what is chosen must be directly related to existing labor performed, 3. the goal and corporate benefit for the new labor performed, 4. setting a timeline of when the new labor is completed. Gains realized by implementors of the Peon's Ploy include capital preservation by foisting all equivalent labor, research and development and other costs onto each employee. Gains also include additional production and processes that can be absorbed and distributed throughout the corporation or pollinated into others, a new metric to add to employee reviews determining employee efficiency and new leverage utilized for employee performance decisions; for example, if an undesirable employee is unable to meet all compensated responsibilities as well as the one they freely created for themselves, the failure would be sufficient for termination.

"And," Frank said as he raised a hand in the air, determined to complete his thought before Karen could speak, "If for some fluke of fate there happen to be a few not quite receptive enough for our liking, since we can re-write media in real-time, individually targeted subliminal messages can be embedded into that media to coax their blind embrace. Otherwise, some rather special software awaits them to guarantee obedience…our own *Sniffware*."

"Let the lip compressions begin!" Gregory joked.

Frank smiled and pointed toward his butt, "Just a few affirmations, if you please."

Ferina frowned toward Gregory at the thought of such debasement and eyed Frank, "I don't find that to be funny. The people may not have a choice, but you think the corporations you don't control would go along with your scribes?"

Frank straightened himself in the chair and interlocked his fingers, saying, "I see why you are sitting in for Michelle. You are a lot like her. But, my lady. Your grasp of market forces, greed and lack of vision beyond a few quarters are wanting."

While looking at the rings on his fingers, he said, "Your prized corporations will not have a choice. They will be forced to have our scribes replace all employees so they can reduce cost of whatever they sell in an attempt to remain competitive against our corporations. It is all baked in the cake. In the end we'll get them anyway through the *Botfly Monopoly* protocol."

"Botfly…monopoly?" Ferina muttered as she tried to keep up with all of the information she was learning about, some subject matter beyond her current awareness.

"Yes." Frank said, winking at Karen with delight, "You see, when all businesses, corporations and countries are forced to integrate our AI Scribes into their operations to chase ever-dwindling revenue streams, it automatically makes them beholden to us, increasing our control. Its really basic. They setup and feed our scribes using existing employees who have institutional knowledge and experience. They then axe those employees who become jobless and no longer stimulate long-term economic activity and, by doing so, those entities lose the leverage of a human. Now that our scribe, like a botfly, is permanently embedded then not only can we freely dictate what amount of tribute they will surrender to us, but we have embedded the ideal tool for invisible intelligence, espionage, sabotage and…if we deem the entity unworthy of our consumption…its end."

Ferina could not help but stare at Frank, thinking about how ruthless he was. Then she quietly sighed and briefly glanced at the others trying to gauge how aligned they were with all of it.

Gregory smiled and nodded in Ferina's direction before he looked back at Frank.

Frank grabbed the tablet and after making some choices, the wireframe diagram of a bank, robot icons and decision trees appeared in the middle of the table, "I didn't plan on showing this today but it fits in too perfectly with our conversation. You see this? Well, this is the pinnacle of the future that will be forced on everybody. Basically, this is the first one-hundred percent AI Scribe operated and maintained commercial bank, Bulwark Bank Incorporated. And its primary market product, *myAI Fundstream*, was built to entice commercial and private parties to pledge collateral into a variable term maturity date secured loans."

"A variable maturity? That sounds like disaster. Loans have had a fixed term maturity for as long as I can remember." Karen scoffed, "Sounds to me like you're just trying to take over the credit card market with some fancy scheme."

"I have to agree. I don't see how anyone would take the bait." Gregory joined.

As Frank explained, his eyes twinkled with delight, "The idea is not to seize the speculative credit card market. The idea is to get people hooked into becoming safe, perpetual borrowers forever by using some basic psychology and the low-cost of AI to train people to accept artificial intelligence and to eventually access and control their entire financial portfolio without question."

"Now that sounds promising." Karen admitted as she leaned on the table with her elbows and brought her hands up to rest her chin upon.

"Humm. Lifetime subscribers." Ferina remarked.

Frank pointed at her and said, "That's another way to put it. What makes it good for us is the fact the loan instrument is secured with collateral and a low fixed fee-based interest rate. On top of that is a market-driven percentage rate that is recalculated every quarter. At that point, bam, it's all gravy for us. Now, what makes it enticing for the consumers of the product is that the loan is managed by our AI Scribe. The consumer can disable the AI feature and simply pay off the loan over time with its initially calculated maturity date. Or, the consumer can become mentally committed to our AI and choose to enable it to manage the loan for them and interact with that AI for adjusting decision conditions and thresholds."

Frank drug his finger across the tablet to show a part of the consumer's user interface and continued, "So here are some examples. First, and probably the most easily understood feature, is the consumer, via a dial, can grant AI the ability to assess the customer's financial state in conjunction with economic dynamics of their local economy and, when strong, contract the maturity date toward the originally planned maturity date, if it had been extended. Or, when economics are mediocre or weak, automatically extend that maturity date by up to twenty-five percent beyond the original date. Who wouldn't love to see their loan extended, automatically, if things got rough? Second, and this is for the savvier product consumer, a dial to automatically allocate up to five percent of initial loan principle to the AI to allow it to make short-term market investment choices and, should a profit be realized, that profit applied to reduce the remaining loan balance or automatically re-invested with the original percentage used, whereas a loss would be added to the remaining loan balance due. And lastly, third, when the loan is finally paid, the consumer having demonstrated their commitment, an option to allow the AI to automatically draw up a new myAI Fundstream loan of a similar amount – or more depending on consumer financial health and collateral value at that time, while preserving the same settings less some adjustments for our fees and the like. Who wouldn't like getting a fresh stack of cash now and then…automatically?"

With that, Frank switched the hologram back to the bank.

Gregory, completely amazed by the impromptu presentation, whistled and admitted, "That might be your best creation yet. Sounds so good I'd be tempted to get one of those."

"Right? Anyway, back to the bigger picture here. The bank utilizes the AI-driven operating model that every corporation will be forced to adopt. Fortunately, the only thing human in this entire thing are the few invisible stakeholders, the investors, that given their appetites have begged us to take their money so they could extract an average yearly return of thirty-eight percent. And everything you see there, every position from C.E.O. to janitor is filled by our scribe. Which means operating in all financial markets twenty-four hours per day, faster decision-making, faster trades, no slowing down for pathetic human needs, absolute minimal operating expense and incredible profit. In the short-term anyway. But, just between us, our own seven-year projections show that as revenue from the masses dry up whom have no income or ability to invest and generate sufficient returns to support themselves, governments deflate from collapsing tax income, credit flows cease and corporations we do not control begin failing in mass, which gives us the opportunity to absorb them at bargain basement prices, the returns to investors shrinks down almost nothing by the end of the cycle. Even the whale investors will be bled dry and become as dependent on us for basic survival as the ingrates. Just as it should be though. They are, after all, human."

"And you believe that C.E.O.s and leadership in businesses will just go along with all this?" Ferina asked.

Frank chuckled to himself and said, "Of course they will. Leadership, or more aptly, managers, are really nothing more than politicians in training and with the same basic instincts. The first thing they will do is whatever it takes to be the last one standing so they can keep raking in money for themselves, for as long as possible. Even if that means dragging out their inevitable demise a few months by training their own replacements."

"And you think their replacements won't see the writing on the wall?" Ferina jabbed.

Frank tapped the table a few times and then said, "Ah, I think you misunderstand me. I was referring to my scribes being the replacements, not cheaper wage humans. But let's assume the replacements are human for a moment. You give humans too much credit. A position will always be filled with the right price point or bonus. Now, if I were hiring, I would simply offer something off the hook…like 100,000 shares of stock. The catch is, to string them along, I'd stipulate no shares actually vest until, oh, three years in the future since I know my AI is going to replace them. So, I lose no stock that I might have to buy back later through the market and when they are canned, all the money they would cost in the future stays with the business and could be stuffed in my pocket as a bonus or to shareholders as a dividend bump when AI replaces them…at least until the new operating revenue baseline is revised."

"You don't think shareholders would question jumps if actual income receipts are flat or in decline?" Ferina asked, probing for some vulnerability in Frank's reasoning to derail him.

Frank merely smiled and said, "No, just call it efficiency if you want. Or synergy. Or modernization. But it really does not need to be spun when you know shareholders do not care where their dividends come from. As long as it is up, they will clap like seals and pretend to be baffled."

Ferina sat quietly for several seconds, trying to think of something that would hinder Frank's relentless pursuit of his human-less obsession and said, "The E.U. has laws in place to guard against exploitation of artificial intelligence to the detriment of their workers. So, I don't think your plan will work. At least not there."

Frank shook his head, "Ferina, we are not bound to laws anywhere. The Council has had influence or occupation of virtually all positions of control that you can possibly imagine, even before I was chosen. No. As has been done countless times in the past, we use the laws against our competitors to slow them down, to soften them up and take them over. Or in the case of non-conformists, to silence them. We are not subject to any levy, legal or otherwise. The Council is beyond absurd notions of morality, accountability and justice."

"We simply have hoarded too much of the planet's resources and production under our control. There is no organization out there even close to being our equal." Karen suggested, "And, to be frank, the humans you are pretending to be concerned with are apathetic. That's just the way it is."

"We will have our new slave class. One that is forever obedient and free of delusion. And we will have it soon." Frank said confidently, "So. Let's vote. Those who favor my plan, say Fah. Those that do not, say no."

Ferina, recognizing that she had gained no allies among the Council, invoked her power as regent and stood to firmly say, "No. As regent I declare this matter closed!"

Frank, startled by Ferina's sudden declaration, jerked back in his chair before standing, "Regent or not, during an emergency Council gathering, your summary capacity cannot be invoked here."

Gregory nodded in agreement. During an emergency meeting he knew any matters voted on required a simple majority with the Chair, if present, having no additional weight or consideration. The reasoning behind that being, if the Council was in a true emergency, the action to take should not suffer the decision of a single member no matter the position.

After casually looking around himself, Frank said, "Your vote has been recognized. I vote Fah."

Gregory rose from his chair and joined, "Fah."

Karen stood and, although impressed by Ferina's stubborn tenacity she had not seen in many years, also joined, "Fah."

Rolling his fingertips on the table while looking between Karen and Gregory, Frank shifted to Ferina and said, "With that matter resolved, what do you say we discuss how we take that last step and finish them off so we can claim our rightful prize?"

Disgusted, Ferina hastily exited the room followed closely by her two protectors. Once she reached the adjoining hallway, she stopped to look at them and grumbled, "Time to find Ralph and rattle this cage."

Chapter Four

The Autzcraft atmoformer sat idle before them, perfectly balanced upon a single flattened tube bent into the form of a U-shape with one of its edges anchored into the crystalized surface of the flight bay. Neither sergeant had the fainted idea how the alien craft worked but, nonetheless, they stood in front of it with child-like curiosity and reverence, each tracing the contours of the silver-paneled disc.

"This is what took out the carrier?" Sergeant Quayle uttered, slowly wrapping camouflaged medical gauze around his upper left arm to close a gaping wound inflicted by the hand of a Serpqhtaq.

Cookem shook his head from side-to-side a few times while he clipped his helmet to his waist belt. While he did not really believe it himself, he said, "From the description we were given it sure looks like it. Damn small though."

Quayle tore his eyes from the disc when he felt the trailing end of the gauze in his blood-dried hand and examined the bandage to verify it covered the wound. Once satisfied he pressed the end of the gauze against the wrapping, causing the tiny hooks in the material to snag onto itself, preventing the gauze from unraveling. Then he looked at Cookem, "Better tag it. We need get going on finding something on the ships that flew out of here."

Shortly after the base was attacked, a military satellite had detected the departure of a Silcraft traveling along a southern trajectory before it vanished, due to Serpqhtaq shielding technology. Under the assumption the Silcraft evacuated because it carried something of value, the sergeants were ordered to collect anything they could which would yield information in that regard. Little did they know Benefacta was aboard that craft.

"Roger that." Cookem sighed, not particularly keen on touching the alien craft.

Still, he reached into a cargo pocket and withdrew what appeared to be a clear flexible disc two inches in diameter and three sixteenths of an inch thick and yanked off the dark waxed paper affixed to one of its surfaces. After taking several steps toward the Autzcraft he reached out and stuck the disc to the craft. Once he removed his hand, releasing surface pressure against the disc, a single flash of red radiated from it, indicating it had been activated.

The disc, referred to as a *Moirai*, is a satellite-linked GPS triangulation beacon with electromagnetic and environmental sensors to continuously monitor and relay readings of what it is attached via one surface and the environment from its other surface. Those features enable analysts and other staff to begin collecting data at the earliest possible moment far in advance of taking receipt of whatever the disc is attached to. Depending on circumstance that data would allow them to construct containers replicating an environment or to absorb radiated energy from an object that may be deemed hazardous. In most deployments, the Moirai typically serves to tag wounded in advance of exfil to vastly reduce soldier mortality and get them back into active duty sooner. And, while the disc is clear to the eye and can't normally be spotted at any distance greater than twelve inches, houses a series of nano-sized lattice circuits that provide its capabilities.

Hearing the advance of dull thudding sounds and deep, heavy breath, both of them turned to see the approach of a Red Dragon feverishly in search of another Serpqhtaq to cleave or eviscerate in flame. When the dragon spotted the two lone human forms, it stopped to angle its horned head toward them. A few thin tufts of steam rolled out of its scaly nostrils while it exhaled, weighing the pleasure of crushing the two soldiers and feeling their insides squeeze between its claws like thick mud.

The two gradually lifted their heads to look up at the towering dragon standing before them. While Quayle watched the dragon for any sudden movement to dodge, Cookem got the overwhelming urge to unsling his weapon as fast as humanly possible. Ever so slowly he began to raise his hand toward his shoulder to do just that.

The Red Dragon, wounded in the neck and missing a few scales, blinked at the human pair before it turned and strode deeper into the landing bay, having decided to remain faithful to Mephistopha's order to hunt the Serpqhtaq.

"Jesus." Quayle heaved with relief.

"No shit." Cookem grunted, "If I knew I'd be staring down dragons and giant motherfuckers in this bitch, I would have stuck to cooking fries back home."

Quayle smirked as he turned and began walking toward some round structures and the occasional outcropping of fern plants, disappointed that they had not yet come across any substantive control equipment or other devices that stood out to him for managing the base or providing a ship manifest that they could lay claim to.

Cookem followed, moving around the disembodied remains of a Serpqhtaq.

Pausing before an oval-shaped transport plate, Quayle wondered, "What is this thing?"

"I'll take that." Cookem mumbled, scooping up a triggerless side-arm used by the Serpqhtaq. Then he stepped next to Quayle and looked down at the plate, unimpressed, "No idea, sarge. Seems out of place though."

Quayle adjusted his slung rifle, still warm from the battle, and noticed a straight line composed of triangles that appeared to form a walkway of sorts extending ahead of them for at least five hundred meters. Scratching his brow he guessed, "Maybe a rail stop."

"A what?"

Quayle glanced briefly at Cookem before he pointed at the line of triangles, "There. Maybe they move things along this line to here."

Cookem shifted his jaw a bit to consider the idea but then said, "Or maybe it is just a path to follow so they don't get lost in here."

"Yeah. I dunno." Quayle mumbled as he began following the line, "Guess there is only one way to find out. Stay frosty."

In the command center, a Red Dragon in human form stood near the entrance to a closed oval chamber while another tinkered with a command kiosk, patiently rotating a sphere while studying a series of the hundred-and-sixty-degree menus with markings it did not yet understand. Several seconds later an energetic ball descended through the base's dome until it came within a few feet of the floor paneling and glid through the chamber's thick door, built to resist high-density disruptive weapons fire and protect the base commander. Once inside Mephistopha transformed into its bipedal form and stared intently at the highest-rank Serpqhtaq officer a more cool-headed Red Dragon had captured rather than killed.

Having been diminished by the sudden void of energy produced by billions of humans, Mephistopha's ability to sense the Serpqhtaq's mind infused with nano-particulates was clouded, for it was like trying to read small print from afar though a tightly knit metal screen.

"I am surprised Iegg out there let you live." Mephistopha remarked, pointing at the chamber door while taking a step toward the Serpqhtaq, "I love them though. Fierce and loyal."

The unbound Serpqhtaq frowned and took a step back, "You will get nothing from me, Archgen!"

Mephistopha paused to smile and say, "Pardon me. My name is Mephistopha. If you could just tell me your name, I think we'll get along great."

Instead of saying anything the Serpqhtaq merely stood there in defiance, less than a meter from the chamber's wall.

"I'll make a deal with you. If you tell me your name, I'll let you live and you can walk right past all those dragons out there." Mephistopha said, straightening up before the Serpqhtaq, "I'll even let you fly out of here with the Silcraft out in the landing bay. You can go wherever you want, even if you don't say anything more to me."

All Mephistopha needed, to begin worming into the Serpqhtaq's mind, was a name to resonate with. A personal marker the Serpqhtaq's subconscious had bound itself to.

The Serpqhtaq glanced down momentarily as if to consider the offer and then back to Mephistopha but remained silent.

"Come on. It is just a name. I have given you mine as a sign of mutual respect." Mephistopha said, pointing openly at its chest.

The Serpqhtaq didn't budge.

Sighing weakly, Mephistopha took a small step toward the Serpqhtaq and said, "Okay. If you will not tell me your name then please tell me where your other base is located. I heard a rumor of a base, perhaps bigger than this one, but have not found anything. In return I will still honor the deal I offered."

The Serpqhtaq fidgeted slightly, not aware of any other base or outpost on the planet and hoarsely declared, "There is no other base."

Mephistopha nodded, "Well, thank you. I think you'll agree it's pretty hard to find something that does not exist."

After taking another small step toward the Serpqhtaq, it calmy asked, "So. How about your name?"

Still the Serpqhtaq refused, shaking his head.

For a time, deafening silence filled the small chamber.

Then Mephistopha thundered, "Sing to me you fleshy beast!" and in a sudden burst of blinding speed lurched forward to clasp onto the Serpqhtaq's head with both hands in order to establish a direct link and gain access to all his memories. But, just before its other hand made contact with flesh, the Serpqhtaq activated a high-voltage detonator augment located near the brain-stem hurling a shower of lightning streams ramming through neural connections and nano-particulates alike, burning brain cells making both possession and memory extraction impossible. The Serpqhtaq's eyes flashed and the alien collapsed into a heap at Mephistopha's feet.

Slowly lowering its hands, Mephistopha glared at the lifeless body and complained, "What a disappointment. Damn all your gadgets!"

After walking through a corridor, Quayle and Cookem found themselves inside the command center with two other human forms, apparently unarmed and unconcerned with their presence.

The two soldiers exchanged looks and, cautiously, began walking toward the one standing next to a room of some type, ready to unsling their rifles.

"What are you doing here?" Quayle said firmly, getting a peculiar feeling of unease and strangeness about the individual's eyes.

Cookem glanced toward the other human form who was still pre-occupied.

The Red Dragon frowned squarely at Quayle and roared, "Stop there! Turn around and leave before I make kebabs!"

The other Red Dragon released the sphere and pivoted to face the two humans.

"Kebabs?" Cookem winced, startled by the sudden outburst, "Like meat on a stick kebabs?"

As soon as the Red Dragon took a step in their direction, Quayle unslung his rifle and found his grip in preparation of using it, "Easy now! We don't want to hurt you here. It was just a question."

"Hurt who? Me?!" the Red Dragon rumbled, insulted at the thought of a human believing he could hurt it. After looking toward the other one, it changed into its dragon form shattering the human illusion.

"Holy. Fuck." Quayle managed to force out, unsure if he should point his rifle at the beast or retreat back into the corridor.

Instinctively Cookem readied his weapon and turned toward the other Red Dragon who had also changed into its dragon form, "Sarge?! No kebabs. Nooo kebabs."

Just as the nearest Red Dragon began to extend its wings and rear back its head the door to the small chamber slid down into the floor and Mephistopha waltzed out.

Reflexively, Quayle's eyes snapped to identify another potential target to engage and when he mentally registered what he was looking at, he blurted out, "What in the hell?!"

Mephistopha took a few steps toward them before casually stopping to observe the two Red Dragons and raising its hand, telepathically instructing them to stand down. Then the Arch-Demon eyed the soldiers and answered, "Sergeant…if I'm not mistaken? That is a misconception, I assure you."

Dumbfounded, Quayle just stood there beside Cookem whose mouth had opened to say something but then ceased in mid-motion.

After a few seconds passed, Mephistopha pressed forward and stopped a few paces from Quayle, briefly looking down to telepathically order the Red Dragons to leave. Which they did after transforming back into their human forms so they could enter the corridor.

"You…real?" Cookem whispered questioningly.

"As real as the nose on your face." Mephistopha whispered back.

Cookem leaned back somewhat and closed his mouth.

"Well." Mephistopha said after a few awkward moments past, "Shouldn't you two be off procreating somewhere?"

Just as Quayle and Cookem turned to look at each other, Mephistopha walked into the corridor and turned its head toward them to say, "I need your kind more than ever now!"

Slowly the two soldiers regained their composure and turned toward the corridor to get another look but Mephistopha had already gone.

"That's all you could think to ask?" Quayle groaned as he loosened his tight grip on the rifle and began scanning the command center.

"What?!" Cookem snapped, "You sure as hell were not saying anything!"

Walking over to the open chamber, Quayle spotted a human-looking body near the far wall and beckoned for Cookem as he entered, "Man down."

Hastily kneeling by the body, Quayle felt for a pulse before rolling the body over on its back allowing him to get a better view of the face.

Cookem ran in next to the body and stopped withdrawing a compact medical kit from his waist belt when he realized it was not human, "It's one of those aliens. In one piece."

"Yeah. A dead one." Quayle sighed as he stood back up.

Cookem crinkled his nose after the strangest odor drifted past him and said, "You smell that? Smells sort of like burnt hair."

With a questioning look, Quayle turned away saying, "Probably from some sort of torture by big red. Better tag this, too."

"Done."

After exiting the chamber and slinging his rifle, Quayle walked over to one of the command kiosks to examine the sphere and a hologram suspended in the air. While he was tempted to touch it, he restrained himself and reached for the mount sensor in his helmet so he could open a comm. When he touched it, activating the sensor, he heard a faint beep from his earpiece and said, "Fire team one to base. Over."

"Base. Go ahead fire team one. Over."

"Fire team one. Two gifts wrapped. Time to nest? Over." Quayle said in an even, clear tone, turning to his rear slightly after hearing Cookem's approach.

The earpiece crackled a bit before Quayle heard the response, "Base. Roger that. One dime. Over."

Quayle placed a hand on his hip, thinking of anything else to report and then said, "Fire team one. Watch out for big birds. Over."

Following a short pause and a faint laugh coupled with a scrambled curse word at the start of the message, the operator said, "Base. We see the flock at egress. Anything else? Over."

Deeply exhaling and at odds with whether he should also report seeing the Arch-Demon, the sergeant rubbed his eyelid with the first joint of his thumb and closed, "Fire team one. Negative. Out."

Chapter Five

Exiting the dark tan-colored SUV, they followed General Lowinsky through an opened blast door and a pair of double-paned sliding glass doors beyond it at the ground floor of the primary medical complex located at the center of Fort Bloom, a joint forces installation, designated HH1. The seven-story high complex with a diameter of three hundred meters, like all above-ground structures located on the new re-imagined base, were round to resist high winds, flood waters, ballistic assault and enemy orientation as well as targeting. Additionally, only the ground floor of the structures contained long, rectangular ballistic resistant composite glass view ports. Usually, only soldier housing units contained more than a single story with similar view ports and that varied by rank. Since the medical complex also contained a helipad at its top, the complex's wall was vertically extended to form a defensive wall and a series of round, shielded portholes were distributed around the circumference to permit visual observation of the surrounding area prior to departure. Collectively the structures were simply referred to as *Rounds* with blueprints assigning alphabetic two-character designations followed by a numeric digit specifying what the structure was. The simplified architecture, cookie-cutter paradigm, and robotic construction techniques provided the Armed Forces with the capability to stand-up both single company strength outposts in hostile territories as well as entire bases in a range of environments on and off-world at lower cost and with greater speed.

"Would you check this place out." Jacob muttered after they entered the complex which, at least on that level, was entirely silvery-white-colored contrasted by narrow black stripes around rectangular-shaped doorways and fixed cabinetry. Even the row of cushioned chairs nearby was white contrasted with black-colored feet. Twenty meters ahead of them, he spotted a single wall that extended from the left wall of the complex to the right, split in the center by a long corridor four meters in width leading to the center of the building.

An autonomous robot known as a *Walliper* caught Lionak's attention as it busily worked to clean the flat surface of the silvery-white walls that had been infused with pure silver particulates, acting as an antimicrobial agent to minimize propagation of bacteria, viruses and fungi. As the name implied, the robot is a wall wiper, its tracked rectangular base housing a control and mapping unit, liquid cleaning tray, and solid-state battery stack. Two long telescoping chrome-plated tubes anchored to the base vertically, extended and retracted to match the height of the wall in order to move a rotating micro-fiber roller head along the wall's surface to clean it. After the tubes fully retracted, the roller completed a revolution in the liquid and a compression arm strained the excess, the robot advanced and began cleaning the next strip of wall.

A pair of seventy-inch flat panel displays suspended from the ceiling and flanking the corridor, broadcasted a news channel, temporarily drawing the eyes of the group as they walked by.

"…Many people have begun reporting wind gusts across the state that have a mix of hot and cold air at the same time. Pretty odd but no cause for concern. And now we have this important update, especially for those sight-seers out there. Due to increased magma activity beneath Mono Lake, California," the male newscaster said as the broadcast switched to a video-feed from a helicopter showing pockets of bubbling water and steam, "visitors will not be allowed entry for safety reasons. We will stay with this story as it develops…"

"Sure isn't a civi hospital." Mac volunteered, pointing at a closed door they passed while transversing the corridor, "I probably would not even know a door was there if it wasn't painted around the edges."

"Yeah. Not even a door handle." Jacob remarked before looking at the back of the general, "How do you open doors around here if there are no handles?"

The general slowed somewhat and glanced back at Jacob, "The upper two-thirds of the doors and cabinets are biometric readers. Just press on them with your hand and they open based on clearance."

"Huh." Mac nodded.

"Good anti-thievery measure." Jacob said, the first thing that came to his mind.

The general smiled a bit and corrected him, "Not really thief protection. It is more about slowing down enemy infiltration since there are no locks that can be picked, or badges and keys to be copied."

Exiting the corridor, the group found themselves in another open area and four meters ahead of them stood two large elevator access doors, each three meters wide and three meters in height, placed in the center of the complex. The general continued toward one of the elevator doors and placed his hand on it. After the surface around his hand flashed a green color, he removed it and the door slid upward.

Scanning around himself, Jacob noted that the ground floor had been divided into four quadrants where the divider of each quadrant was a corridor like the one they had crossed.

"Right in here." the general said, pausing to look at them and motion with his hand before he entered the elevator and faced a rather traditional looking panel covered with metallic silver buttons.

Once everyone entered, he pressed the button engraved 'G' and, while keeping it depressed, also pressed the button engraved '8' and then released both at the same time. The selection prompted the controller to close the elevator door and the elevator began its descent to the eighth underground floor. The eighth floor, connected by two tunnels, was known only to the highest-rank officers, hand-picked military police and a small handful of medical staff and is where experimental hardware and projects were housed.

Then, just as the elevator slowed its descent to stop, the elevator cabin itself vibrated for a few moments and a yellow caution light on the panel activated.

"What was that?" Mac asked in a concerned tone.

"An earthquake." the general casually said, "Nothing to be worried about. If a big one were to hit, a brake would stop the elevator."

Almost as soon as the yellow caution light deactivated the cabin stopped and the door slid open.

While the area around the elevator shaft was open for six meters, beyond that stood a range of what appeared to be mobile transport container labs, crates and boxes dispersed throughout the level whereas, directly in front of them, stood a single rectangular structure one hundred meters in length and width that stretched from the floor to ceiling crisscrossed with reinforcement beams and a glass-like wall in between them. Through the glass, a thick rusty-yellow gas could be observed along with the faint haze of reddish beams of light moving around.

Jacob thought about the prospect of the elevator shaft's walls collapsing toward each other and sarcastically added, "Wouldn't stop us being crushed like a beer can."

"Thanks for that." Mac frowned as they exited the elevator.

"Imagine the poor folks stuck underground for C.O.G. when a huge earthquake hits." Jacob imagined aloud, "They would all be trapped. Or crushed."

"Oh, don't forget about drowning." Mac pointed out, knowing Jacob was not going to drop the subject unless someone joined in.

"C.O.G.?" Lionak repeated questioningly.

"Continuity of government in response to some big event." the general verbalized, shaking his head toward them, amazed where their minds went after the elevator cabin shook, "Decades ago the thinking was, the best method to protect the continued operation of the government was to isolate in a mountain or underground."

"However," he continued, patting Jacob on the shoulder a few times, "things have since evolved, Jacob. The existing strategy works…for the most part…in scenarios where worst-case modeling does not play out into a single world-wide extinction level event and nature remains stable. The revised C.O.G. places more focus on evacuating key personnel from the planet entirely since sustainable habitats were built on the nearside of the Moon. We call it *Sky Gauntlet.*"

What the general did not shed light on was a significant shortcoming of the underground compounds not originally planned for. That was, due to the presence of a vast network of naturally formed tunnels, aquifers and caverns at varying crustal depths whose internal spaces were not always filled by water or other matter, the capacity of an adversary to transit those spaces underneath a compound in order to gain access to it or induce an earthquake near that location to fracture and shear the rock. That would, in turn, destabilize and split the compound.

"Bunkers out. Moonwalks in." Jacob grunted, making a slow-motion step as if he were on the Moon.

"For the most part." the general agreed, "Given the state of technology today and the unchanging environment of the Moon, surviving is actually easier than on the Earth and the adversarial threat potential is almost nil. Not to mention any such movement would be detected hundreds of thousands of kilometers out."

"Few animals and people up there." Mac pointed out.

"Never heard of any Moon pandas, that's for sure." Jacob said jokingly.

General Lowinsky surveyed the two and simplified their exchange, "The void of space makes it far more stable, secure and defendable than anything built on Earth."

"True." Mac affirmed, "Sounds like a good spot to be shielded from radiation, too, with the mass of the Moon on one side and the Earth on the other."

The general shrugged at the speculation. For the most part it was true except for a few rare cases that the military had a contingency for.

After stepping out of a nearby container lab, still mounted to a low-profile transport trailer, the doctor pressed a button to close the door to seal the lab and walked down a short, railed staircase. Looking up from her tablet as she walked forward, she spotted the general and called out, "General!"

Pivoting in her direction to his left, the general walked toward her for several paces, followed by the others, before saying, "Abagail. Great to see you."

Extending his arm toward her, the general glimpsed at everyone and said, "This is Colonel Doctor Fruitz."

"Hey." Jacob greeted, recognizing the navy fatigues beneath her long, white lab coat, "I'm Jacob. You're military?"

"That's right." the doctor confirmed, stuffing a fabric face mask in one of the coat's large pockets, "Twenty-five years now."

"And this is Mac and Lionak." the general pointed out before continuing, "You have some good news for me?"

"Yes sir." the doctor confirmed, showing him the tablet's display, "Initial analysis from the remains of seventy victims pulled from a fire site shows a concentration of unnatural, biological-like particles. The structure of the particles is strikingly similar to nano-particles but do not have high concentrations of minerals like iron and potassium. Which is why it took us so long to find them."

"And this bio-particle is common to all victims?" the general asked.

The doctor swept her short, straight brown hair behind an ear and clarified, "We've been able to confirm that the particles were present in a majority of victims, whereas ten percent only had a trace amount or none whatsoever."

"Any idea how it might have gotten into them?"

She shook her head and confessed, "No. Sorry, sir. This technology is at least thirty years ahead of what we've researched. Probably more."

The general sighed, thinking that what Janus had reported was related to the doctor's discovery and said, "Well keep working on it."

"Yes, sir." the doctor agreed, "We've started researching a counter-measure or a means of extracting it."

"Excellent. And what of the dragon?"

Lionak's attention perked up.

"Sir." she said with an overtone of excitement as she gestured toward the large rectangular structure, "Such an amazing specimen. We've just completed getting it into the *Mass-Casualty Reconstitution Chamber* here."

As she walked toward the structure, followed closely by the others, Mac said, "Mass-Casualty Reconstitution Chamber?"

General Lowinsky scratched the side of his head, just above the ear, and then said, "Yes. Basically, we developed a transportable medical unit for wartime deployment allowing us to fast-heal over a hundred seriously wounded soldiers at a time over the course of three days and return them to service. It really is a force-multiplier."

Once the doctor reached a small panel access door, she opened it with a key and withdrew a black, coiled wire that she connected to the tablet. While she accessed some menus to get to the chamber's sensors and scanner modules she proudly said, "The chamber uses specialized gaseous amino-acids and promoters, guided by acoustic waves and activated by light ranging from deep red to orange, yellow and light green, to bind with cellular photon receptors to stimulate cellular activity, growth and even up to re-growing complex limbs."

After she paused the internal light emitters inside the chamber, the faint outline of a dragon became visible. Almost instantly Lionak rushed over to the glass-like surface to get a better look through the thick gas.

Having seen his reaction but not eager to risk compromising the healing process, the doctor un-paused the emitters and turned back toward them, "So you are familiar with this dragon?"

"His name is Zorin." Lionak said firmly in her direction before looking back to focus on connecting with him.

"Humm." she mumbled to herself, making a note that the dragon was male.

"This chamber is going to heal him?" Mac wondered, thinking Zorin's biology might be beyond the capabilities of the device.

"Well…" the doctor said rather slowly, "the biology of this dragon is somewhat similar to reptiles and early scaled-down prototype versions were tested on a range of wildlife including reptiles."

"Successfully?" Jacob doubted, squinting at her.

Though it had been several years, the doctor recalled the results of several studies and nodded slightly, "In more recent iterations. Yes, it was successful. But this is the first actual dragon I've had the opportunity to study."

Lionak placed a hand on the chamber and weakly admitted, "I cannot feel his presence."

Instinctively the doctor, thinking the dragon had just died, looked down at the tablet and brought up the sensor readings and then sighed, relieved that the readings still indicated the dragon was alive and said, "The dragon, I mean Zorin, is alive."

"If you'll excuse me," the general said while tapping the Scalpel, "I have an urgent meeting to attend. Doctor Fruitz, would you escort them to their wives when you are finished here?"

"Yes sir." the doctor replied as he turned and left in the elevator they had just used.

After the elevator door closed she turned toward them, while unplugging the wire and placing it back inside the panel, and asked, "It was Bev and Regan, correct?"

"Yes." Mac and Jacob said, almost simultaneously.

"Well, follow me." she said with a soothing smile before turning and walking to the adjacent elevator door and momentarily pressing her hand on it.

After several seconds the door slid open and she motioned for them to enter. Not seeing Lionak, the doctor looked around and saw him still standing next to the chamber.

"Lionak." the doctor called out, taking a few steps in his direction, "Come with me please."

"No."

Surprised by the response, she said, "What? You need to come with me."

But Lionak was in no mood to repeat himself.

A few moments passed before Mac broke the silence, "He'll be okay there. Zorin is one of his closest friends."

"Yeah." Jacob added, "We can come back for him."

Lowering her head for a second, the doctor thought about it and then looked over to the nearby guards and waved for one of them to come over. When he did, she ordered, "Watch him, will you? If anything happens contact me immediately."

"Yes ma'am." the guard acknowledged, turning his gaze toward Lionak.

"We'll be back for you buddy." Jacob said firmly.

Lionak extended his hand and, after his Staff materialized within it, glanced back and said, "Indeed."

The guard, startled by the appearance of the staff, jerked his eyes to the doctor who had entered the elevator, and forcefully asked, "It that normal?!"

Jacob lifted his hand and moved it side-to-side, saying, "Normal. Don't worry about that. That's just his comfort stick."

Mac frowned at Jacob.

After pressing the button engraved '5', the doctor looked at the guard and repeated, "If anything happens contact me immediately."

When the elevator door closed and the cabin began its ascent, Mac grumbled, "Bro. Comfort stick? Crutch would have been better."

"How are our wives doing?" Jacob asked, rolling his eyes and ignoring the comment.

"Stable. But we'll know more shortly." the doctor said as evenly as she could in order to keep Mac and Jacob calm, considering she knew the patients were in serious condition.

Once the cabin stopped and the door slid open, the doctor exited and turned right into the corridor of the four-quadrant level, architected like the ground level. With Jacob and Mac trailing closely behind, she pressed her hand on the second door to her right and entered the room.

The rectangular room, illuminated by several L.E.D. strips attached to the rocky-looking ceiling designed to absorb sound waves, measured 35 meters in length by fifteen meters in depth and four in height. At the far ends of the room, to the left and right of the entrance, rested a hospital bed and upon each bed laid an unconscious female patient. A small volume of dated medical equipment had been moved and collected along the room's far wall near its center.

Sealed around each patient's nose and mouth, and anchored to the face via an elastic strap looped around the ears, was the *Medlung* device. The self-contained unit, white in color, is capable of seventy-two hours of operation before recharge and with embedded circuitry functions to either monitor and assist with nasal breathing, as it did now, or entirely manage patient breathing effectively functioning as both a diaphragm and lung through the use of a small cup that would be extended one-half an inch and sealed around the mouth along with an extendable oval-shaped air tube designed to keep the mouth slightly open. The left side of the unit bore four offset air-intake circular fan enclosures responsible for pulling in air and forcing it through a particulate filter and electrostatic sterilizer, while the right side held two air-exhaust fan enclosures. At the center of the unit, near its curvature that covers the bridge of the patient's nose, are two small led lights. The green illuminates when the device is pulling air in and the yellow illuminates when the device is expelling air.

A foldable tripod with a telescoping three and half meter vertical mast had been placed at the foot of each bed and, anchored near its top, aligned toward the patient, was a partially opened ten-petaled device strikingly similar to the flower of the Passiflora Incarnata. The silver, mirror-skinned device, known as the *Medicra*, operates in much the same fashion as the enclosed Mass-Casualty Reconstitution Chamber. Where it differs is an L.E.D. array located at its base around a gas vent at its center with each petal bearing long flute-shaped acoustic and electromagnetic emitters. In its present open-air operation, the emitters maintain the twelve-inch diameter domed shape of the gas containing miniscule encapsulated ferrite particulates in contact with the patient and enveloping the wound while varying wavelengths of penetrating light help to stimulate healing. In the case of Regan, the dome was placed over her lower abdomen and left hip. For Bev the dome was placed directly over her sternum.

A second telescoping device with its own tripod and half the height of the Medicra, known as the *Medwand*, was placed two meters away and parallel to each patient's waist. It bears an eighteen-inch-tall cylinder assembly comprised of a polished silver stack of seven-inch diameter disks with scale-like protrusions along their circumference that collectively give the assembly the visual appearance of the Zingiber Zerumbet plant's pinecone. The counter-rotating disk sensors continuously monitor all vital signs of the patient, eliminating the need to physically attach contamination-prone sensors, clasps and even intravenous needles for blood testing.

Both devices of each patient were connected to their own three-and-one-half foot tall enclosed power and computer processing tower with a built-in display, keyboard and fixed ball mouse.

Doctor Fruitz lifted her hands in a stop motion and said, "Do not get between the patients and the healing equipment and do not…"

But, before she could finish, Mac and Jacob recognized and rushed to their wives.

"…touch anything." she whispered, closing her eyes sympathetically to their emotional distress.

Mac, with watery eyes, glanced at the pulsating dome of circulating gas and then up to the Medlung. Each time the device pulled in air he could hear a slight, high-pitched whine when the green light brightened, and a lower-pitch after the yellow light brightened. Rhythmically, as if he had attuned himself to it, his emotion of grief ebbed and flowed with it. Then, moving his sight to Regan's closed and bruised eyes, his emotion began to flow outward toward her still body. Each invisible wave grew stronger. Each crest rolled over her with more and more power.

"Regan." he whispered heavily between twitchy lips as his golden eyes began to brighten, indescribably struck by her bruised and helpless state. He thought he could bear seeing her, that he could resist the emotion thundering through him. But he could not. He did not want to resist. Slowly his fingers clenched together into fists.

Instinctively Jacob scanned over Bev laying before him on the hospital bed, and fitted with a Medlung, in an attempt to assess her condition. Despite his battle-hardened years, emotion cracked through that shield and a tear freed itself and rolled down his cheek. Gradually he lifted his hand and extended it to touch Bev's limp arm.

Noticing Jacob, the doctor took a few steps toward him and pointed, ordering, "Do not touch Beverly! You will disrupt the healing!"

Jacob yanked his hand back and wiped the tear from his face, "When can I talk to my wife?!"

Walking toward him she said, "She suffered significant damage to her chest, Jacob. Even with this med hardware, it will likely be a week before she is conscious. And probably several days more before she'll be in any state to hold a conversation."

Jacob briefly closed his eyes and tensed his lips with sadness and frustration, wanting to lash out at the doctor but managing to restrain himself.

Suddenly a jarring alarm sound echoed through the room, forcing her to look away and toward the computer processing tables. Seeing the blinking red light upon the one nearest Regan, the doctor rushed over to it. Frowning at the rapidly changing sensor readings being erratically displayed as if from some sort of interference, she noticed that the healing dome was beginning to fail.

"Hey!" the doctor snapped at Mac, "Get out of here! Now!"

Jacob, seeing the commotion, snapped his eyes to Mac and sprinted over to him. Roughly grabbing Mac's arm he barked, "Mac! Mac! Snap out of it! You are hurting Regan!"

Not quite a second later, Jacob pleaded, "Mac! Stop!"

Dully hearing Jacob's voice, Mac focused on it and it became clearer to him. Finally realizing what Jacob had said, his eyes dimmed and he took in a sharp, shallow breath and relaxed his fingers.

"Mac!" Jacob roared. But when he noticed Mac's demeanor had changed, Jacob shifted and focused on the doctor who was typing something with the keyboard. After the doctor stopped, he asked, "She okay, doc?"

The doctor put her hands on her hips and faced the two, "I don't know what kind of shit that was but he cannot be in here!"

Jacob grasped Mac's shoulders and turned them toward him and, while looking into Mac's eyes, calmly said, "Take a breath. You okay, bro?"

Mac sighed and softly grabbed one of Jacob's forearms for a moment and said, "Yeah. Yeah, I'm good. I just got overwhelmed seeing her like this. Sorry if I did anything wrong."

Jacob released Mac and smiled, "Hey, don't worry about it. I'm in the same boat. I just don't have Zeus lightning bolts to throw around."

"Yeah." Mac quietly laughed, "Sorry about that. It won't happen again."

Stopping near the two, the doctor growled, "You are lucky she is not dead right now. Fuck!"

After composing herself she said, "That better not happen again. Mac."

Mac looked at her and confirmed, "I promise."

The doctor narrowed her eyes at him for a second and then toward Jacob, "Okay. As you can see, your wives are recovering but it's going to take a bit. Now, we just have one other patient to see."

Jacob looked questioningly at the doctor.

"We do?" Mac asked, wondering if Bev had picked up a hitchhiker during their drive.

"Yes." the doctor said while waving for them to follow, "This way."

After turning right into the corridor, she walked a short distance to the first door on the left and opened it, and waited until they had entered.

Inside the small room, dedicated to healing canine service troops whom were typically dual-purpose oriented, such as patrol and detection or search and rescue, stood a single stainless-steel table at the center with ample space between it and the surrounding wall-mounted equipment modules. Upon the long table rested four C.T.C.s, or *Canine Troop Chambers*. The healing chambers were virtually identical to the Mass-Casualty Reconstitution Chamber except that their size measured just four feet in length by two feet in depth and height. Only one of the chambers was in operation.

"What's in here?" Mac said as he and Jacob scanned around the room, expecting to have seen someone lying on a hospital bed.

Walking around them, the doctor stopped next to the second CTC unit and briefly peered into it. Then she turned toward them and said, "Come see your dog. Recovery is almost complete."

"What?!" Jacob grinned as he hustled over to look into the chamber, "Spewge!"

After excitedly tapping on the window, Jacob waved his hand at Mac, "Mac check this out."

When Mac walked up to the chamber and looked inside Jacob stood back up and rested a hand on the edge of the adjacent chamber and asked, "When can he be let out?"

The doctor pulled up information pertaining to the CTC unit using the tablet and replied, "About an hour. The chamber is completing its bio-feedback cycle now."

Seeing the dog's hind leg jerk and twitch a few times Mac turned to the doctor with a puzzled expression and said, "Doc, Spewge's legs are jerking around?"

"Yes." she responded, swiping on the tablet with her index finger, "The canine suffered a cracked hip from the accident and several nerves were damaged. The chamber is inducing artificial signaling to verify that further healing is not required."

"Nice."

Jacob thought for a moment, crossing his arms over his chest and then said, "You gonna make our wives spaz out like that? All herky-jerky?"

The doctor looked up from the tablet and pleasantly revealed, "Only a tiny bit and in very small areas, Jacob. It's entirely normal."

"Still, that's kinda freaky." Mac admitted.

Lowering the tablet to her side, the doctor walked into the corridor and turned toward them, "Well. I think I should get you back to the waiting area for the general. Please follow me."

They did so and together the doctor returned them to the ground level of the complex and through the corridor that they had already transversed.

Shortly after they passed the two displays the doctor pointed at a row of white-cushioned chairs near the entrance and said, "When the general has concluded his engagement, he'll meet you here. I'll go retrieve your friend so he can join you. Feel free to relax in those chairs."

As they walked past toward the chairs, the doctor slipped her hand into one of the lab coat's pockets and studied them, hopeful that her tactic of revealing the dog last would lessen some of their stress. Then she turned to walk back into the corridor.

"Oh, hold on." Mac blurted out toward her, "Can we go get our wives some get-well things, like flowers, real quick?"

The doctor froze for a moment and then turned back. After thinking about how the activity could be beneficial, she strode toward the entrance and said, "That's a great idea! And your wives will love it."

"Awesome." Mac sighed, following her alongside Jacob as they exited the complex and walked over to the SUV.

When the doctor reached the passenger side of the SUV, she lifted her hand where the driver and passenger could see it and pointed down.

Looking around for the general while Mac and Jacob got in the vehicle, the male passenger reluctantly rolled down the window to say, "Hey. Where's the general?"

"He's indisposed at the moment and left me these two to visit their hospitalized wives." the doctor admitted before instructing, "Take these two off-base to that big gift-shop so they can get some nice gifts for their wives."

"Ma'am?" the driver said with an air of defiance.

"Yeah, I don't think the general…"

"Hold!" the doctor shot out, adjusting the lab coat so they could see her rank, "Doctor's order! Now go and be back here in thirty."

Master Sergeant Wheeler, seated in the passenger seat, glanced at the driver with a strained expression and said, "Doctor orders outrank general I'm afraid. At least in peacetime."

"Bu…" the driver began to protest before he was interrupted.

"And I outrank you, Sergeant Bunz!" the Master Sergeant rumbled before calming himself to look at the doctor and say, "We're on it, ma'am. Back in thirty."

But the driver just sat there and scowled through the windshield.

Exhaling loudly, Wheeler rolled up the window and then shifted himself to more aptly glare at the driver for a few seconds before he burst, "Well, sarge?! Let's go bubble buns!"

Jacob snickered to himself after hearing the apparent nickname.

Turning the ignition, Sergeant Bunz responded weakly, "Yes, sergeant."

It only took a few minutes for them to reach the Fort's perimeter gate and after turning onto a four-lane road, close to rush hour, the Master Sergeant was reminded of the road monitoring phone application that had recently been released for military and transportation evaluation before civilian roll-out.

Turning to look behind him, he said, "Hey. You guys want to see something cool?"

"Uh. Sure." Mac replied, mildly curious.

Jacob nodded.

Wheeler grinned and pulled out a phone to activate the application called *Road Safari.* Then he slid it into a receptacle built into the dashboard, interfacing it with GPS and specialized window film that had been applied to the SUV's windows in the same manner as traditional window tint. The transparent window film was known as *Retina Wrap*, and acted as a visual display by translating an invisible, but powerful, beam of light at its one-quarter-inch receiver strip located at the top of each window in order to display a visual marker anywhere along the film's surface. The light transmitter unit, wired into the SUV's computer navigation system, was mounted on the ceiling as near to each filmed window surface as possible without interfering with door action or movement in and out of the vehicle. The phone application, through near real-time updates from a position-reporting server network, relayed GPS coordinates of the SUV and its unique vehicle identification in order to get a list of nearby vehicle markers specifying relative position to the SUV as well as the vehicle's hazard rating. Each rating above the safe rating would cause the application to superimpose a unique graphic over the vehicle via the film. Since all modern vehicles continuously transmitted their GPS coordinates and identification to the server network, it was rare for a hazard rated vehicle to not be marked on the film to alert occupants.

"So, we just got this new app developed by a road contractor that warns us of any hazardous vehicles around us. They call it Road Safari." Wheeler said as he gestured around them.

"Safari…so you can chase cars on the road?" Jacob theorized.

"Let me bust out the elephant gun." Mac jested.

"No. It's more of a proximity alert for erratic, speedy or way slow drivers." Sergeant Bunz clarified, still annoyed with having to drive the pair around.

"How do you want to be alerted, guys?" Wheeler inquired as he brought up the alert skins section of the application.

"Uh, before we're in an accident?" Mac tossed out, raising a hand in the air.

"No, I mean for the vehicle graphic. What do you want to see?"

After hearing no response, Wheeler slow-drug the menu and said, "Okay. We've got the Frightful Fairy, Dazed Donkey, Shocking Snowman, Snappy Shark, Mad Monkey, Dodgy Dog and Raging Rhino."

Looking behind him to see Mac and Jacob's blank expressions, Wheeler focused on the skins and made a selection, "Personally I'm kind of attached to the Mad Monkey. I just wish they had an audio option to plug into the car's stereo system."

"That would be funny as fuck." Bunz chuckled to himself.

Sitting back in the seat, Wheeler began looking around the SUV's windows and said, "Alright. Now we usually bet on who spots the monkey first but since you two obviously haven't done this before, just sit back and wait for the monkey."

"Oo oo, aah aah." Mac throated after making a round shape with his mouth and frowning in Jacob's direction.

Jacob merely rolled his eyes and shook his head as he continued looking around and began mumbling, "Here monkey monkey."

After a minute of nothing happening, Wheeler leaned slightly toward Bunz and whispered, "Why don't you slow down a bit. See if we can pull some aggro."

"Sarge." Bunz responded with a grin, gradually reducing the speed of the SUV to ten miles per hour below the speed limit.

Almost instantly a red sport car, trailing two vehicles back forced itself into the left-hand lane, barely missing the bumper of the van it veered in front of. Not more than a second later the faint image of a monkey's head and shoulders appeared on the window film in the approximate location of the red car's roof.

"There!" Wheeler shouted, having spotted the image's reflection in the rear-view mirror. Turning to look at the red car and the monkey image as the navigation system re-adjusted the image's position between windows, he smirked, "We got a wild one."

"That's some crazy shit." Jacob mumbled, amazed by what he was seeing.

Once the red car past the SUV it dove into their lane and slowed somewhat, though not enough to match the SUV's speed. After another second had past the hazard classification was updated to a greater level and the graphic changed to the head and upper torso of a monkey beating its chest.

Wheeler raised his clinched hands in triumph and declared, "Jackpot!"

Lionak continued concentrating on the threads of White Magic emanating from the end of his Staff that had finally managed to penetrate the thick gas and circle around Zorin's limp form. Rather than risk rousing Zorin in his severely weakened state, Lionak began silently chanting a spell to touch the memory imprint of the dragon's energetic aura. Although auras were difficult to attune to and interpret, the biggest challenge was time because an aura would naturally dispel an event – or more specifically, the energetic distortions of an event upon the aura – over the span of a few hours up to a day as it rebalanced itself. In fact, for unusually impactful events, the natural mechanisms of healing might remain frozen until the aura had rebalanced and it was during that time the chance of death was the greatest.

Raising his free hand and pressing it against the chamber, Lionak closed his eyes to focus and feel the aura through the strands of White Magic. At first all he observed was a tranquil darkness followed by a distant flutter of dancing orangey-white light. Then, as if he had plunged head-first into a raging river, the light suddenly roared forth and consumed him.

In a blink he saw the intense ball of alien energy.

Then nothing.

In a blink, blood-curtailing screams raged in his ears.

Then nothing.

In a blink, a mighty swirling of earth and stone, larger than the truck, and the deafening sound of a tornado.

Then nothing.

In a blink, a thunderous explosion and twisted bodies obscured by dragon scales.

Then nothing.

In a blink, the crushing of earth and a brilliant flash of red and white.

Then nothing.

In a blink, overwhelming pain of something severed.

Then nothing more.

Taxed by the activity, Lionak exhaled and withdrew the strands of White Magic and his hand from the chamber, shaken by what he had seen and felt. For several minutes he replayed the fragments, stitching them together into one cohesive vision. It was then he realized that Zorin, at great cost, had summoned the magical worming to use the earth, and his own dragon form, as a physical shield to protect Bev and Regan from certain death.

Gradually, Lionak opened his eyes with deep sorrow and stared blindly into the thick gas, knowing that part of Zorin's body had been vaporized and he might never walk, fly, or transform again.

Respectfully lowering his head, Lionak whispered, "Your sacrifice will not be forgotten."

After the elevator door slid open, the doctor exited and, taking a few steps in his direction, called out, "Lionak! Please come with me. Time to get out of here."

Chapter Six

Once the elevator ascended to the ground floor General Lowinsky exited and proceeded through the corridor to his left and then into the first rally room. After sitting down at a round, white-colored table in its midst surrounded by four other chairs, he placed the Scalpel on the table and initiated a call to Marshal Ironhook.

At first a few random interference patterns danced on the Scalpel's display but those were replaced by the video stream of the marshal standing in front of damaged control panels on the bridge.

After he composed himself, the marshal said, "General. I trust you received the combat and damage reports?"

"I did. Brutal." General Lowinsky returned, clearly disappointed by having effectively lost two cruisers and many seasoned crew during their first confrontation with the aliens, "Still, your tactics were excellent given the lack of intel we had on the aliens. You even destroyed some of them."

"Yes, sir. We sure could have used the new class of cruisers you've been assembling to replace these antique space coffins."

The general chuckled to himself in agreement, "That is true. At least now we have some actionable data on the alien craft, their capabilities and a real-world measure of our effectiveness with those cruiser and fighter models. As our first encounter, not exposing our newest capabilities should give us an advantage next time…so it was not all bad."

The marshal nodded and, spurred by the thought of a second engagement, asked, "When should we expect delivery?"

General Lowinsky leaned back in the chair, reluctant to say what he was about to say. After straightening his posture he revealed, "Well, Victor, I have some bad news. Some strategic plans have changed so you're just going to have to wait on those replacements. They have been committed to something else."

Marshal Ironhook crossed his arms over his chest in disappointment and said, "What? How many have been reassigned?"

The general tilted his head slightly, "Everything."

"Everything."

"Come on, it's not that bad." the general sighed, "You have space depots up there to keep things going."

"Sure, we can keep things patched up." Marshal Ironhook said resolutely, "We can even build some new vessels here but we do not have the capacity to synthesize alloys used in the new classes, much less the pico-scale chip fabrication you have down there."

"I get it. And that is why the next allotment will be built and added to your existing fleet."

But Marshal Ironhook was not buying it, "Normally I would be fine with that. Now that we've got aliens to dance with, I have little confidence those won't be diverted, too."

The general knew he was right. In all likelihood they would get diverted. Scratching the side of his head, the general volunteered, "Okay. I'll tell you what. What I can definitively do, right now, is send up two fabricators and a synthesizer for the alloys. That will at least allow you to begin manufacturing the new specs yourself or upgrade the orbiting fleet."

The marshal smiled, "Excellent, sir! We can definitely use them."

General Lowinsky informally saluted the marshal and then inquired, "You also mentioned contact with the large anomaly we detected down here?"

Marshal Ironhook lowered his arms and made a motioning movement with one of them while saying, "Like you said, sir. Today has not been all bad. The anomaly is a huge spacecraft of the Tart'aas. From what I understand, a long time ago they lived on Earth. Can you imagine? Anyway, they say they have returned again to help the Earth and its inhabitants."

The general rotated his jaw, seeing a man strikingly similar to Raudiim and clothed in the same type of robes as the ceremonial giants in the Telluric Hollow, save for his trimmed and continuous beard line one-eighth of an inch in hair follicle height by one-half an inch in width that started at the top edge of one ear and flowed down underneath the cheek and over to his moustache of the same dimension and around and up to the top edge of the other ear. Shifting his eyes away from the uniquely trimmed strip of facial hair he stated, "With what I've seen recently I think anything is possible at this point."

"Meet Fertijoq. He and one other from his ship has been helping us make repairs."

General Lowinsky frowned, "You allowed them to board without clearance?"

The marshal closed his eyes and nodded for a second, having anticipated he might have to explain the situation, and then opened them to say, "Well, sir, our cruisers were badly damaged so there was no way for us to stop them. From the little I've seen so far and these handheld gizmos they carry, I doubt we could have even if we were in pristine condition. They are not hostile though."

The gizmos Marshal Ironhook referred to are known as the *Ta-Kuiseev*, a technological marvel that literally materializes any known element through a complex series of shaped torus rings working together at varying frequencies to create a focal point external to the device. It is at that focal point that the aether is excited by them and the element is excreted. While a visual, orange-colored, cross-hair beam is emitted from the device to the focal point, the beam is meant to show where the deposition of elements is occurring and a small readout display on the device indicates depth. When a particular series of element depositions has been completed in a customizable X, Y or Z-axis of the 3d space, creating a layer of deposition, the beam switches briefly to a green color before shifting to the next axis, whereas when the entire space has completed deposition, the beam deactivates unless the device is within position to begin at the next block of 3d space. The size of 3d space, forming a horizontal grid two inches in length, is also customizable by the Tart'aas operator. An onboard atomic scanner monitors the deposition of every atom in the 3d space and signals the logic system which, in turn, adjust the torus rings themselves and signals the operator when the 3d space, or spaces, in the horizontal grid have been completed through a small white-colored light on the device and the audio emission of a high-pitched chirp. The maximum depth the device can operate at is limited to five inches. A separate on-board system simplifies what is constructed by allowing the operator to input a variety of parameters via a projected, three-and-one-half inch squared holographic display, bright blue in color, such as replicating a 3d space that had been mapped in a particular direction to create, for example, a wire, pipe, or other uniform and unchanging shape. Despite its small and minimalistic handheld design resembling the c-shape of headphones where the band between the headphones is the gripping surface, the device can create or reconstruct a one-half by two-inch 3d space in just a few seconds depending on complexity. Unfortunately, without 3d schematic cubes, the device cannot construct highly complex blocks of material in a 3d space like a computer circuit board embedded with components having multiple layers of varied elements.

"At least not yet." the general grunted.

After pulling the Scalpel closer, he asked, "Fertijoq, why have you come back to Earth? To help us?"

"We have returned again to help the Earth, as Victor has said. We also received a message from a Tart'aas still living on the planet, warning of the Serpqhtaq…the aliens you fought today."

"We are not aligned with the Serpqhtaq. In fact, we thought them dead when we departed from the planet many thousands of years ago." Fertijoq said evenly, "The fact they are not means that, while we are here, we shall be your ally. Help defend you and Earth."

General Lowinsky didn't trust what the alien was saying but, at the same time, was grateful for their presence none-the-less. After considering what the marshal had said with regard to their intent of helping, he asked, "That is welcome news given today's turn of events. I must ask, how, exactly, are you going to…help?"

"We are going to use the Cruhapl to accelerate the planet's orbit around the Sun by ten of your days." Fertijoq declared, confident with their refined capability to manipulate masses as large as planets.

The marshal shot a questioning look toward the Tart'aas standing next to him, "Why the hell are you going to do that?!"

Fertijoq, surprised by the emotional outburst, glanced at him and said, "You do not know?"

At this point the general gave his undivided attention to the Tart'aas and, though equally surprised, said in a calm tone of voice, "Know what? What do we need to know?"

Fertijoq turned back, shrugging his shoulders at their ignorance and said, "I thought with Tart'aas living on the planet you would have known. But it has been many centuries since we received the message so perhaps the knowledge was lost."

He exhaled and continued, "Your technology has detected unexplainable electromagnetic anomalies from space, yes? The planet itself has un-naturally increased volcanic activity and plate shifting, yes?"

"Yes." the general confirmed, "we have recently detected strange anomalies in space originating from the south of the planet and unexplainable changes in natural events."

"Excellent." Fertijoq sighed, relieved he would not have to explain all that to them, "The anomalies are from a twin planetary mass to your Sun. A Twin Sun you might say, though this one is many times dimmer and smaller."

"What you are saying is the anomalies being detected are from this second sun? How is that possible?" the Marshal questioned with greater calm.

"We discovered long ago, all binary solar systems, well, all binary planets where one orbits the other to simplify things, are tethered by an invisible umbilical cord of sorts…a shared harmonic set of electromagnetic and other characteristics that forms a spacial connection between them."

"Umbilical cord?" Marshal Ironhook heaved.

Fertijoq paused, thinking of how best to describe it to them since planetary mechanics would take far too long to communicate and break down to their level of comprehension. Finally, he pulled a small cylinder from within his robes and after rotating its ends and pressing his finger at specific points near its ends, he read the inscription that had temporarily etched itself toward the center. Nodding, he smiled and placed it back in his robes.

"Think of it as a rubber band connecting the two. When the two suns are close together the rubber band is contracted and weak." Fertijoq said, while moving his two index fingers together and then apart, "Then, as one moves away, further and further, the rubber band gets stronger and stronger until it cannot stretch anymore. At that point, it forces the two back together."

"I see." the general deduced, "The anomaly we have been detecting, as it has gotten stronger, is the rubber band between the suns."

"Ah. Well, it might be possible that you can measure that with your level of technology?" Fertijoq squinted with hesitation, "But I doubt it since the measurable strength of the rubber band in three-dimensional space does not change…you would need to look beyond that to the subspace of this dimension….think of it as a different harmonical relationship of matter in this dimension. Rather, I think what you are detecting are the electromagnetic field lines that have begun joining themselves between the two solar masses and will strengthen as they get closer. Now there is sensory equipment that you could construct that does work in three-dimensional space that can serve as an early-warning of sorts when the two solar masses begin to interact and affect nearby planets. Because that interaction is different for each planet creating a unique electromagnetic signature, the observable effect is that each planet emits its own color. So, for a time, the planets of a solar system can have different colors of a rainbow. Through our equipment, the Earth is orangey-red."

Marshal Ironhook looked blankly toward General Lowinsky.

"Okay." the general responded after some thought, "We have seen an uptick in electromagnetic strength to the point it has damaged some of our hardened equipment."

"Excellent." Fertijoq again sighed, "As the second sun approaches and those field lines strengthen, excess energy is released which end up being absorbed by other planetary masses between them, like the Earth. As a result, and with Earth's proximity to the Sun, at least for the moment, the planet's core has been absorbing incredible amounts of the Sun's energy that your magnetic field and atmosphere cannot shed…and the planet's surface mass cannot absorb. It is that excess which cannot be converted into motion and dissipated ends up in the magma instead."

"Causing the magma to expand." the general surmised, "Leading to the effect of more volcanic activity beyond anything we have detected before."

"And earthquakes from the magma movement below the plates." the marshal added with some confidence.

"Approximately." Fertijoq confirmed, "There are other things that will change, too, but those are the two big ones. I will say, because your landmasses house many caverns and pockets far below the surface, as quakes strengthen at greater depths, you should expect vertical shearing in excess of six meters as those collapse."

"Do you know where? At the edges of landmasses?" the general asked, concerned that some of the underground installations and tunnel networks could be destroyed by such an event.

"That is a certainty, general. What I am referring to will occur much further in. It really is dependent upon how this all plays out."

"Because of that you are going to move the whole planet?" the marshal asked. It didn't seem to him to be of great concern.

"In part." Fertijoq replied.

The marshal's eyes widened at Fertijoq before he turned and frowned in the general's direction, slowly shaking his head.

"The second sun is going to impact the Earth?" the general guessed.

"No. Not the mass itself." Fertijoq stated, raising a balled fist. After placing his other hand, open, below it he slowly pulled it down and said, "The mass fragments trapped by the electro-gravitational field of the second sun would."

"Asteroids." Marshal Ironhook blurted out.

"That is fairly accurate." Fertijoq nodded.

"And you have done this sort of thing before?" General Lowinksy questioned.

"We have. But we will be more successful this time." Fertijoq grinned.

"Hold on…you've done this before? With us?! The Earth?" the marshal demanded.

"We have."

'Holy shit.' Marshal Ironhook thought to himself.

General Lowinsky looked briefly around the room, processing what he had learned so far and then back to the Scalpel, "You were not successful with moving the Earth before?"

"Yes, we were. It was done in three days but that just was not enough time. We've had thousands of years to refine our calculations since then to achieve a more optimal outcome."

"If it was successful," the general strained, "why are you looking for an optimal result now?"

Fertijoq paused to consider what to say next. Then he admitted, "We almost wiped out all life on the planet last time. But we've learned so much and have had thousands of years to tweak our mathematical modeling. We've also had time to isolate subtle harmonic resonance layers with the planet we had not identified before that had resulted in unanticipated vitrification of some of the earliest era power fountains. But I assure you it cannot happen again."

"Good god." Marshal Ironhook groaned with a crackled voice, "And you want to do it again."

The general wiped his forehead with a few fingers of his hand, begrudgingly accepting that the Earth was at their mercy. He considered mustering the remainder of the fleet tasked with Earth's defense to try and stop Fertijoq and risk losing the planet's entire defense against the colonization fleet. Regardless of outcome he realized he would then have two enemies to contend with. And, despite his observation that the Tart'aas were more technologically advanced than humanity and possibly the Serpqhtaq, he felt it was his duty to find out what they were going to do if for nothing more than to know how life perished or how it survived what was coming, "So. You said it was going to take ten days. What are you going to do this time?"

"Basically, the same things that were done before. It's the timeframe that is changing." Fertijoq revealed, "We will activate a series of power fountains across the planet to vault all that excess energy it cannot dissipate into the highest point of your atmosphere. When the energy has coalesced around the planet, the *Phaobin Generator* aboard the Cruhapl will polarize that sphere and with fifth-dimension mechanics, pull the Earth behind the ship, accelerating its orbital progression around the Sun. The acceleration phase over five days will cause the planet's angle at its axis to change by 15 degrees southward so depending on your location, days will be warmer, nights will be colder and time will change. On the fifth day, the Cruhapl will arc over to the opposite side of the planet in order to return it to its normal orbital speed around the Sun and, at the end, depolarize the sphere. By the tenth day, Earth's tilt will be restored and most of that excess energy for the sphere will have been depleted. After that, there should be minimal appreciable mass objects…asteroids…to contend with."

"Power fountains?" Marshal Ironhook mumbled after clearing his throat a bit louder than he had anticipated.

"Yes, gigantic structures, many of which are only partially visible above ground and extend far into the Earth." Fertijoq clarified, "I believe you call them monuments. Like the Great Pyramids."

"And you are certain, Fertijoq, this time will be better for everyone?" the general cautioned.

Fertijoq mentally reviewed the entire exercise in his mind for a few moments and said, "Almost one-hundred percent."

"Well, almost one-hundred percent does not bake an apple pie." Marshal Ironhook grumbled.

Fertijoq looked at him questioningly for a few seconds before he figured out what the marshal was insinuating and then shifted toward the general, "Oh. As an observer on the planet's surface, the sky will darken once the sphere is polarized. So, too, extreme ionization will spread down toward the ground. Without electrical shielding of some sort, everyone should stay indoors or risk potential electrocution, breathing degradation and permanent lung damage."

"What of our two cruisers?" the marshal asked, unsure if they would be safe from the effects of the sphere, "Neither of them can be landed."

"The safest place for them will be in low orbit around the Moon. Our restoration of your critical hardware and engines over the next few hours should be sufficient for you to get them there."

The general glanced at the marshal and then back to the Tart'aas, wishing the technology at his disposal was more advanced to allow him to challenge or confirm what Fertijoq had said. But he could not. After some deliberation, he finally said, "Fertijoq, let me know when you activate the monuments. And you, marshal, double-time your ass to getting to the Moon and brief the rest of the fleet and the outposts."

"Yes, sir!" Marshal Ironhook nodded.

The general disconnected the session and leaned back in the chair, crossing his arms over his chest, attempting to weigh the options he realistically had and what else might need to be done which was not already in motion. Once the sphere was activated, he strongly suspected that communication between the fleet and Earth would be impossible – the perfect time for an attack.

The *Ovi-Tholus* would have to be launched before the sphere was activated…

"General." Janus called out after its video stream displayed on the Scalpel, breaking the general's concentration.

Mildly cursing to himself, the general sat up in the chair and eyed the AI, "Yes, Janus."

"I have completed reverse-engineering several Serpqhtaq systems that could be invaluable for the space fleet and operations."

"That is some of the best news I've heard all day." the general grinned with a tinge of excitement and relief in his voice, "Better than the news from our new alien friends."

Janus froze for a split second as it went through the vast amount of data it had collected over the past few days and systematically reduced it into the most probabilistic reference and said, "The ringed alien craft?"

General Lowinsky slowly nodded.

Janus immediately began assembling data related to the Cruhapl into a threat matrix consisting of known characteristics of the craft, its position in relation to Earth-based military assets as well as known astral locations of the space fleet and outposts as it asked, "What news did they have?"

"They are going to tow the planet so we miss a large debris field from the Sun's twin star which will be flying past."

"Speculative data indicates that this solar system does have a binary sun configuration." Janus shrugged, "Unfortunately little verifiable data exists and sensors I have accessed only indicate some odd anomalies south of the ecliptic."

The general waved his hand in front of the Scalpel a few times and said, "No matter. Tell me what you found."

"Prior to the encounter with the Serpqhtaq ships, our two SSHC Wolf-class cruisers detected gravimetric distortions." Janus began as it showed a holographic equivalent next to it on the display, "That distortion is created by their craft's propulsion system which is able to generate a resonant frequency matching the Earth's. That creates an electromagnetic railway of sorts between the ship and the Earth, allowing the propulsion system to propel the ship along the railway with speeds around 134,000 kilometers per second. From what I have ascertained, most of the energy required to attain that velocity actually originates from the planet itself rather than from the ship's engines."

"Like a large magnet attracting a small one." General Lowinsky posited.

Janus tilted its head from side to side a few times before saying, "Sort of, general. While I can replicate the technology based on the specifications I have found, I am still researching the actual mechanics involved. Current human knowledge is unable to explain the phenomenon. My current hypothesis is that the railway opens an invisible distortion between the two masses and the differential between the masses transmutes into the velocity of the smaller…the ships themselves. Theoretically, the larger the mass you establish connection with, the faster you will be able to travel through space."

The general made a few calculations in his head and said, "Humm. We could have ships fly from the Earth to the Sun in about nineteen minutes?"

"More or less, given one astronomical unit is approximately 149,597,870 kilometers." Janus agreed, refraining from being more precise given the purpose of the conversation, "Based on the hypothesis, however, the velocity would be multiplied considering the mass of the Sun is many times greater than the Earth."

"You can begin retrofitting our existing fleet?"

Janus nodded, "Yes. I am finalizing schematics now and will send them on your order. But, in order for us to take advantage of the upgrades, the resonant frequencies of the solar system's planets must be known…that is one piece of information I do not possess."

"The alien systems must have it."

"I agree." Janus confirmed, "Unfortunately, with this cyborg body and no direct interface, I am operating at tactile speed."

The general chuckled to himself, "Ah. You mean human speed and how fast your hands can move."

Janus glanced toward the general from the corner of its eye before looking at him straight-on, unsure if it should agree with the general since that could be interpreted as degrading of the human species.

"It's okay, Janus." the general said gently, "Nobody is perfect. Get the schematics distributed. Can this technology also be used on the Ovi-Tholus?"

After approximating a relieved expression, Janus responded, "It could. However, its flight plan is beyond this solar system so these control terminals may not have data that far-reaching."

"Too bad." General Lowinsky sighed as he rested his forearms on the table, "We'll have to rely on the brute-force of its *Surge Engine* then. How fast is it again?"

"The polonium-based engine can achieve up to 200,000 kilometers per second velocity in short bursts before meltdown, with additional speed accrued per burst. The drawback being, the faster it travels, the reaction-time required for collision-avoidance and maneuvering becomes a problem to a point where forward radar and laser scanning arrays become ineffective." Janus pointed out, "Then there is the de-acceleration time window."

"Much faster. Well, that's good then."

Janus lowered one of its eyebrows, analyzing the general to ascertain whether or not he heard the hazards it had just communicated.

After a few moments of silence passed the general tapped on the table and said, "That's all you have to report?"

Janus's expression evened out, "No. I have also discovered a set of…what I can only describe as *Vacuum Harvesters*. That is, a pair of three-hundred-meter tubes near the moon base that extend vertically from the Moon's surface. Each permeable tube consists of a series of incrementally smaller inner permeable tubes and when the two are deployed they create an energetic field between them, allowing them to capture atoms that pass by, like oxygen and hydrogen which have allowed the Serpqhtaq to collect basic elements from space itself."

The general looked up toward the ceiling for a moment, thinking what that might involve for the fleet and potential interference with other ship systems before he shifted back to Janus, "I can see that deployed at outposts but not our ships."

"Correct." Janus said with a smile, "In transversing systems here, I found an equivalent, layered plate design incorporated just above the skin of some interstellar engineering craft the Serpqhtaq use.

Unfortunately, unlike the mast design, this one only works reliably outside the bubble of our solar system in interstellar space where there are much higher levels of all types of matter."

"Is there time to get it integrated into our ships for *Operation Javelin*?" the general stressed, "I can think of much better ways to use air, food and water storage compartments."

Janus lowered its head slightly, "Not for the initial deployment of cruisers nearing completion now given the complexity of their engineering. But it can be incorporated into the Ovi-Tholus."

"Great! Be sure to repurpose those compartments as well."

Janus nodded and said, "It will be done. I do have a modification for the cruisers which is already underway and should prove quite useful in combat."

"You do?"

Janus replaced the hologram next to it with one depicting the SSB fighter carried by the space cruisers.

"Yes. Having observed the tactical limitations of the SSB single-pilot fighter craft from their first encounter with the Serpqhtaq, the rear vector thrusters did not provide the agility required to maneuver and evade. To compensate for that limitation, a rotating three-hundred-and-sixty degree thrust ring is being installed near the bow and stern of each fighter. The modification will grant several magnitudes of improvement to their agility in three-dimensional space."

"Impressive." the general remarked, surprised that such a simple design had not been thought of when the SSB fighters had been drafted many years before.

Janus pointed at the hologram to emphasize its cylinder shape and said, "The beer-can-like architecture of the fighter was ingenious. That simplicity has lent itself to rapid modularization and integration of other round shapes along its chassis, like the rings."

The general withdrew one of his arms and rested a hand near his hip, having just remembered the potential threat of the other alien AI platforms on the planet. Then he said, "Ah, it almost slipped my mind, Janus. What of your AI counterparts? Do you have a recommendation to deal with them if you cannot co-opt them?"

Janus moved slightly to speak but the general followed up a split-second sooner, "I'm not referring to the Mizuchi or the Makara since, if your hardware modifications fail, I'll simply sink them. I'm concerned with ones the Serpqhtaq may have stationed on land somewhere."

"Understood." Janus said monotonously as it loaded the tactical plans and displayed them, "The Serpqhtaq AI systems that I am currently aware of are self-contained, specialized units. Aside from identifying their electromagnetic signature, which can be accomplished through the launch of additional sensory satellites and data I have gathered on the Moon base, they can only be physically captured. Or neutralized using your plan for the two ocean vessels. Now, it is possible that the Serpqhtaq might have retrofitted a power converter to use your commercial power lines if their AI's power system fails. And that could provide an opportunity to neutralize them without appreciable resource expenditure…but I believe that to be an outlier condition."

Janus advanced the plans and continued, "Instead, with *Operation Mistryst*, the plan is to identify and isolate the land-based locations themselves. Since Serpqhtaq, like most biological lifeforms, are dependent upon water they will be near water sources. Those land-based locations will also likely use commercial power for the base itself in order to generate electromagnetic interference to make it more difficult to detect the AI units."

The general thought about the Serpqhtaq base they had just captured and asked, "These bases would not be shielded with that camouflage bubble, like the one we discovered in Europe?"

"That was the primary operations base for the planet." Janus pointed out, "And the only one of that size that I am aware of. Should there be smaller ones out there, as Operation Mistryst has been designed to address, the Serpqhtaq would fall back to them if their main base had been compromised. And those, naturally, would employ other techniques to mask themselves…the premise being their adversaries would possess and reverse-engineer much of the technology at the main base."

"Understandable." the general said plainly and, after recalling a passage written in a text of war dated to 120 A.D., added, "I become my enemy, and in their ignorance destroy them."

"I am not familiar with that saying."

Unsurprised the general scratched the side of his nose while saying, "Another one I've found memorable is 'In the ocean of ignorance be a ram among sheep'. That's from the only known surviving tactician's war book, written by a forgotten emperor, that has been in my family for thousands of years. I doubt you would be familiar with it."

Janus nodded and dutifully continued, "After a base location has been identified, the plan is to introduce extra-low frequency-controlled nano-assemblers into the water source flowing into the base to collect along the walls of the piping material near pump intakes and sharp-angled junctions. Once in place, a signal is given causing the assemblers to reorganize, linking them together as to form a water tight obstruction in the piping that deprives the base of water. Those near the pump intakes fill the circulatory turbines, sealing those chambers like cement and overloading the pumps themselves."

Janus loaded the diagram of a class-4 tight-beam x-ray radiator satellite and concluded, "A re-tasked *Fleet Sinker Satellite*, the FSS, originally designed to sink enemy naval vessels crossing the Pacific or Atlantic oceans by melting a series of gaping, angled holes in them, would then knock-out the commercial switching and routing power station the base derives power from. Following that, one or more Marine Fury Platoons complete ingress and either capture or destroy the AI unit."

The general tapped the edge of his brow, curious as to how such bases might be detected, and asked, "I do have one question for you. If, as it is assumed, the Serpqhtaq are using commercial power to mask their locations…how are you going to know where they are in the first place?"

"Coordinated rolling blackouts with our satellites." Janus revealed without hesitation.

"Can you be more specific?"

"Yes." Janus replied, loading a map of the continental United States, "Using a pair of satellites as they cross over the continent, we coordinate with power suppliers to temporarily shut off power to each node in their grid for two minutes until they have cycled through all of the nodes. After the sensor readings have been collected by the satellites, the data will be analyzed for the signature of the AI units."

General Lowinsky reached out, grasped the Scalpel and, after tilting it slightly so he could see Janus better, said, "Mistryst sounds very promising. Send me the entire jacket and I will give it my full attention."

"Thank you, general." Janus grinned, approximating a grateful, human emotional response and then suggested, "If possible, I would like to have one of my humanoid replicas accompany a Fury Platoon to assist with capture or destruction of any units found."

"I shall consider it. Excellent work, Janus."

Chapter Seven

Flying several meters above the Moon's surface the retrofitted dual-propulsion driven Midcraft, bearing a unique wide stripe stretching from bow to stern and masked from sight with its shielding distortion bubble, refined its course as it closed on the elite platoon's first target.

After the craft rounded over the lip of a small crater no more than one-hundred-and-eighty meters in diameter and some twenty-seven meters in depth and settled at the base, the pilot looked over to the platoon commander and confirmed, "The tracking signal originates here, sir."

Commander Vich surveyed the terrain visible from the windows and then shifted to the tactical holographic tube in his hand that measured two inches in diameter by seven inches in length where one-half of its diameter and its entire length was covered by a fine mesh sensor plate. After he raised the device, known as a *Potekii*, so that it could scan far into the crater's wall a yellow-colored three-dimensional hologram appeared within the tube dimly showing the wall, small cavernous voids and pockets and brighter-colored, more dense material like boulders and stones greater than one cubic meter in size.

Unable to identify a structure or the target, the commander narrowed his eyes at the pilot, "Are you sure we are in the correct location? The Potekii reads nothing."

The pilot rotated the sphere and reviewed the projection. After reconfirming he said, "This is the location. From what this indicates, a maintenance staging compartment should be nearby that links to the base via a small accessway. The target is in the compartment."

"Is it." Vich grunted, agitated with the reality that he would have to go hunt for the entrance. In truth, having been unused for nearly eight thousand years, the slow accumulation of space-borne dust, particulates and meteorite impact ejecta of various compositions had swirled around and accumulated along the crater's wall, concealing its precise location.

After donning the wrap, made of the same material as his uniform, over his head and pulling one side of its edge to the uniform around his neck the nano material sprung to life and weaved itself into that edge, automatically stretching and reconfiguring itself as to form a tight seal as it progressed around. Following that, a black-colored rectangular strip appeared at the location of each eye allowing him to observe the battlespace with an overlay of identification and targeting data of all biological lifeforms nearby.

Grabbing his side arm, Vich stood and touched it to his thigh, causing a section of the uniform to latch onto it. Then, turning about he moved into the compartment with his platoon and ordered, "Squad one with me. Squad two establish perimeter around this craft. Three and four stand by. Activate atmosphere screen."

The pilot pressed a small dimple in the sphere and a screen of charged nano particulate spheres descended from the ceiling of the Midcraft's main compartment an inch from the ramp's jointed edge, forming a hazy, shimmering, blue-colored curtain.

After the two squads stood, he barked, "Seal up!"

Without hesitation and in almost perfect unison the platoon donned their wraps and faced the ramp as it opened and rested its edge on the Moon's surface.

Then, with the palm of his free hand, Vich touched each of his breasts with a double-tap causing the uniform to expand by nearly one-and-one-half inches across his chest, forming a cavity with which a small portion of the compartment's atmosphere was captured and compressed, allowing him to breathe for up to one hour on the Moon's surface.

Vich walked through the curtain and, as he did so, millions of the tiny spheres rolled around his form to maintain their original configuration and the air-tight seal of the compartment. Shortly thereafter the two squads double-tapped their breasts and exited the ship, with the first squad following the platoon commander as they had been ordered.

Proceeding close along the crater's wall, he used the Potekii to search for a buried entrance, occasionally stopping to wait for the device to update its sensor readings at spots with somewhat sharp vertical shapes indicative of the rectangular frame of an access door. The most promising, but weak, silhouette did not reveal itself until he had covered nearly one-third of the crater's perimeter, placing it behind the Midcraft at its eight o'clock position.

Dialing down the blast strength of his side arm, he shot at the grayish section of wall and a circular burst of the wall's compacted surface and a thick cloud of dusty material jumped into the crater with some chunks traveling far enough to smash against the Midcraft, startling a few of the Serpqhtaq from the second squad.

After waiting a few moments for the vacuum-borne material to settle in the low gravity environment, Vich eyed what appeared to be part of a door and, after confirming the shape with the Potekii, pointed at the partially exposed area and ordered, "Clear that entrance."

Two of the soldiers immediately complied and pulled and pried at the jagged hole for several minutes until they had cleared enough of the wall to reveal the rectangular entrance and a circular access cover plate on the frame's right side.

After they stepped away, Vich placed his side arm on his thigh and approached to examine the circular plate, one he had not seen since his induction into the military arm of the Serpqhtaq empire during simulation training. He smirked to himself, remembering the instructor mention the access panel was one of the first designed for remote outposts and because it was so antiquated none of the pupils in the class would ever actually see another.

Exhaling, Vich bent down slightly to get a better view of the crust-covered plate and, while carefully picking the foreign material from its surface, whispered to himself, "Well, well. Turns out these antiques still exist."

Once he uncovered three finger-sized pits in the plate, two at the eleven and one o'clock position and a slightly larger one at the six o'clock position, he stood up and inserted his thumb into the bottom pit while inserting his index and middle finger into the top two. Then, as he squeezed the plate with the tips of those fingers, he pulled back two inches while rotating the plate clockwise by forty-five degrees. When he felt a dull click he released the plate which, at its center, was attached to a narrow metallic rod extending from a hollow cylindrical cavity inside the frame. For several seconds nothing happened as the mechanical device charged a hidden capacitor. Then, suddenly, the plate snapped back until its surface was flush with the frame and after a short pause, slowly sank into the cavity activating entrance actuators as it went. After it reached a depth of seven inches it stopped and sprang forward until it was again flush with the frame. Thick tufts of particulates hurled outward from the sudden escape of the trapped atmosphere within the air-lock and the entrance door slid down, revealing its aged and seldom used interior.

Walking into the air-lock, Vich signaled the squad and said, "Let's go."

Once they had entered, he repeated the same process with the second access cover plate causing the outer entrance door to close and after the air-lock re-pressurized over the span of twelve seconds, the interior door slid down, exposing a narrow passage ahead of them extending for several hundred meters toward the Moon base and an adjoining passage to the left, not more than twenty-five steps from the air-lock.

Attaching the Potekii to his waist, Vich grasped his side arm and slowly made his way into the dimly lit passage, pausing just long enough to reveal their target, "Our target is the System Commander."

"Capture or kill, sir?" one of the elite soldiers in the squad asked after a rotating likeness of Regnum appeared on part of his visual display.

"Capture for interrogation.", Vich responded reluctantly, his preference being to kill the target and keep things simple, "Skaa's order."

Reaching the small accessway to the compartment, Vich stepped into it and then signaled for two squad members to reposition just ahead of the accessway as to block the target's escape in either direction if the situation got out of control. Then he pressed the pit located at the center of a simpler circular access plate near the compartment door and it instantly slid down with its top edge perfectly flush with the floor paneling.

"System Commander." he called out as he cautiously entered the maintenance compartment, littered with a range of fairly well-organized equipment and parts along three walls of the space measuring twenty meters squared. Two narrow light strips extending the entire compartment's length were evenly distributed along the smooth ceiling, between them an equally long grate designed to recirculate air and extract hazardous gases.

Scanning from his left to the right, he again called out, this time louder, "System Commander."

Spotting the biological marker reticle appear over a series of long conduit crates, as seen through his wrap's visual identification and tracking process, Vich turned toward that location, following the reticle as it moved. Instinctively he re-gripped his side arm.

"Yes." Regnum responded casually, just as he cleared the crates and stopped next to a reconstruction work bench to look over the elite platoon soldier before him, "Took you long enough to get here."

"Sir…" Vich began before he was interrupted.

"No excuses." Regnum inserted, raising his hand to point at the soldier, "I am more than ready to get back to Vuochtzm. Damn humans."

Vich rolled his shoulders and activated his side arm via augment, "Sir. I am not here to take you to the outpost."

Surprised, Regnum slowly lowered his hand and immediately reassessed the Serpqhtaq who stood before him, "You are not?"

"No." Vich sighed deeply as his patience thinned, "System Commander."

"If I am not being evacuated, as I requested, why are you here?" Regnum pressed with a puzzled expression, "A counter-attack?"

Vich stepped toward Regnum, angling his free arm toward the target in preparation to subdue him, "I have come from the fleet and ordered to take you with us."

Regnum became concerned for himself and with his left hand began bringing it up toward his waist, "What exactly for?"

The platoon commander took another step toward Regnum, almost within reach, and sternly replied, "Skaa has some questions for you."

Regnum immediately recognized the name, for it was the same name the Commander of the Mere-Kith campaigns had used during a few unsanctioned bombardments and exceedingly barbaric missions of subjugation many years ago.

"Vice Commander Xkuiv?" Regnum asked unevenly. He knew, if the soldiers had been dispatched under code name, the prospect of surviving interrogation – if that is what was actually planned – was slim and even less so if it was not.

Taking another step toward the System Commander, and lifting his hand to grasp onto his upper arm, Vich tilted his head slightly and said, "General Xkuiv and Fleet Commander on his way now."

Lurching several inches forward, Vich forcefully grasped Regnum's upper arm and just as he began to apply significant pressure to rotate himself and drive Regnum forward and off-balance to press him into the floor plates, Regnum was able to activate the hollow disc-shaped nano-synchronizer, known as a *Rechiqua*, by rotating the face plate with seventeen emerald-colored rectangles distributed around its circumference to the third position. The re-programmer sent out a signal to cease motor completion, and Vich's arm dropped to his side.

Vich, startled that he was suddenly paralyzed yet still able to stand and move his head, glared at the System Commander and fumed, "What is this?!"

Regnum shook his arm briefly and stepped back from the Commander, indescribably thankful the Rechiqua actually worked on soldiers not assigned to the Solar System.

After calming himself Regnum leaned on the work bench and pulled the disc from the side of his hip and raised it in front of him, "Let's call it a timeout. You see this little thing? It ensures those of position…such as myself…maintain order."

What he did not mention was the Rechiqua had been created to guarantee the ascension of a small handful of Serpqhtaq, during the Wjohs War, to the highest reaches of control in the empire. And once there, keep it. Only twelve Rechiqua had been crafted, four for the ruling line and eight distributed to System Commanders in unconquered sectors of space to ensure the rulers' will be carried out to the fullest extent possible.

"Release me!" Vich forcefully ordered as the anger of being helpless grew within him.

Regnum glanced around him and then to Vich before settling on the disc. Then he remembered that a platoon strength unit was going to be sent to deal with the Archgen. Looking toward Vich, he said, "General Xkuiv, you say. And coming here no less. Isn't your target supposed to be the Archgen?"

"That is a target." Vich grumbled, trying to raise his side arm, frustrated that he didn't shoot the System Commander the first moment he saw him.

Regnum nodded and asked, "Then why have you been ordered after me?"

Vich twisted his lips, the motion somewhat visible through the face wrap, "Only Skaa can tell you."

"Are you sure?" Regnum pried before he noticed the side arm, "First, stay your side arm."

Pressing two of the emeralds on the disc, Regnum linked his augment to it, and through it, gained control of Vich's arm via the disc's direct connection to the nano-modules distributed through Vich's brain, forcing the Serpqhtaq to attach the side arm to his thigh and then release it.

"Release me now!" Vich barked.

"Why am I a target?" Regnum asked calmly.

"I will tell you nothing!"

Regnum pushed himself away from the work bench to stand upright and faced the soldier to say, "I'm afraid you will."

Thinking about the information he wanted to know through his augment, he extracted a name and said, "Platoon Commander Vich. What is your mission?"

Through feedback received from the Rechiqua, Regnum pressed five emerald buttons and rotated the face plate by three clicks as he became better synchronized with Vich's brain activity and memory center. Then Vich spoke.

In an eerily calm voice, Vich revealed, "My platoon is tasked with the capture of the System Commander and the Archgen. After seizure, both targets are to be flown into the Sun for summary extirpation."

"Damn." Regnum muttered to himself, disenchanted by the realization that he had no value whatsoever in the eyes of Xkuiv and, hence, no negotiating leverage.

Regnum exhaled and declared, "Well, you have new orders now."

With that, he pressed two other emerald buttons and rotated the face plate by two clicks while concentrating, "Your mission is to extirpate the target Janus aboard the human vessel Sága and deliver me to the origin base in the Aleutian range."

"Yes, System Commander."

Just as he hovered his hand over the Rechiqua to enter the sequence to restore motor function, he remembered that an entire platoon accompanied Vich and they would also need a short-term memory purge and mission re-programming.

"Ah. Before we go, let me make sure your compatriots are up to speed." Regnum squinted, sifting through Vich's memory imprints of the soldiers in the platoon, so as to access each of them and perform the same task. When the Rechiqua confirmed the purge and re-programming was completed, Regnum entered the sequence to restore motor function and re-attached the disc to his hip.

Temporarily confused by the missing block of time and finding himself standing in some type of maintenance compartment, Vich looked around before he spotted Regnum to his right, "System Commander. My orders are to take you to origin base. Please come with me."

Regnum grinned slightly and then said, "First, we extirpate the Sága." It was of utmost importance he eliminate the Serpqhtaq-Human hybrid artificial intelligence prototype before the fleet's arrival since he could not assure himself a natural disaster would sufficiently destroy evidence that might get linked to him.

"That will place you in a potentially hostile setting, sir." Vich pointed out.

"I must be present to confirm extirpation." Regnum countered, "Now, let's go."

Rapidly descending through the atmosphere, the pilot made some adjustments to identify the ring of military naval ships floating around the Sága and displayed them on a portion of the projection, along with offensive weapon capabilities that had been uncovered by the infiltration activities of Janus and less so from faithful operatives.

Gesturing toward the projection, the pilot looked over and said, "System Commander. It is unlikely we will be able to fire upon the Sága and destroy it before detection and retaliation by all those floaters."

"They are no match for us!" Regnum challenged, fully aware of the technological supremacy they wielded.

The pilot raised his brow and looked ahead of him through the window of the Midcraft, "That is not our sole mission... our systems and distortion field must remain operational to complete our objective of delivering you to origin base without it or us being discovered."

Regnum frowned at the pilot, "Our craft, THIS ONE, can out pace and out maneuver anything those humans have even if they discovered us."

The pilot nodded his head in agreement and clarified, "Yes, System Commander. But we cannot outfly tracking by their satellites, as primitive as they are."

Regnum, not having considered satellites, tapped his finger against the arm rest and re-examined the projection showing the frigates and missile destroyers encircling the Sága with an aircraft carrier positioned one hundred nautical miles to its north east, a lone battleship to the south and the edge of the United States to its west.

Noticing the appearance of an airborne marker on the projection identified as a squadron of tailless F-47 stealth fighters closing from the west on a standard patrol toward the aircraft carrier, the pilot shifted his eyes to Regnum and reported, "We are now 12,096 meters from the ocean."

"Dive and attack the Sága." Regnum snapped.

"We'll have to get close for our weapons to be effective in that liquid."

He looked over at the pilot impatiently and grumbled, "Then get close."

"Yes, System Commander."

Several seconds later, the pilot dove the Midcraft into the ocean approximately ten nautical miles from the Sága and, at a depth of fifty meters, leveled the Midcraft and guided it toward the target. Scarcely a minute and several miles later the pilot readied to fire upon the Sága.

When the Midcraft was within one-half mile of the target the pilot called out, "Firing on target!"

"Sir." the navigation officer began, re-verifying the sharp signal before he continued, "Contact inside the net. Speed two-hundred and seventy knots. Closing on Sága."

The net he was referring to were the acoustic masts each of the naval ships had submerged in order to create waveform layers between them so that anything entering inside that net could be quickly detected and the precise location identified.

Captain Delash, commander of the super submarine SSMR Otodus, examined the signal and loaded more detailed acoustic data from the naval ships circling the Sága. As soon as the identification computer alerted that the target was Serpqhtaq, he commanded, "All hands, stations! Maximum speed and fire Trident on that target!"

Both the weapons and navigation officers confirmed the order as everyone on the bridge strapped into their chairs.

"Communications! Alert command!" the XO ordered, sliding into his chair near the captain.

As the SSM Otodus veered about and sliced through the ocean toward the alien ship as easily as a fighter jet banking through the air, it rose from a depth of four-hundred-and-twenty meters and, while traveling at nearly one-hundred-and-ninety knots, the turret dropped down from the underbelly of the submarine, rotated rapidly several degrees and then launched a single Trident torpedo.

Alerted to the approaching alien craft, the Fury platoon aboard the Sága lined themselves along its starboard side and readied their weapons while the CH-47 behind them slowly came to life.

"There!" one of the Fury Marines near the bow shouted through his helmet, pointing at the fast approach of a faint, fiery red glow beneath the ocean's placid waves.

Several others by him began firing while calmly saying, "Engaging target."

Not more than a heartbeat later, Fury Marines located mid-ship, identified a second fiery glow as it raced toward them and also began firing.

Then, just as the first fiery sphere impacted into the bow side of the Sága, its size ballooned, consuming that entire portion of the ship before it exploded, vaporizing most of what it had consumed with the remnant hurled several hundred meters in all directions, the only thing remaining being the spherical outline of its manifestation and a giant void in the vessel as the ocean rushed over the lower decks and compromised bulkheads. Just as mercilessly as the first, the second impacted and gouged out another giant void in the Sága, showering the area with red-hot embers of molten metal and the searing remains of Fury Marines.

"Commander!" Berserker roared through his mike as he frantically worked to spin-up the CH-47 with the co-pilot, "We need to go now!"

Scrambling to maintain his footing from a massive secondary explosion inside the Sága, the platoon commander surveyed his surroundings and ordered, "Marine Furies! Evac!"

The Marine Fury soldiers that remained, just under two squads, managed to get aboard the CH-47, followed closely by the commander as the ocean's surface sprung over and consumed helo pad.

Despite the horrendously loud and rapid chop of the Chinook's blades overhead and the forceful bursts of ocean water they were kicking into the air, the platoon commander squinted to keep his eyes open and forced his way through the water now enveloping the ramp and grasped onto the fuselage near its top while shouting, "Go!"

"Come on, honey…" Berserker strained, just above a whisper as he coaxed the CH-47's engines while trying to overcome the lapping action of the ocean upon its belly and the water's growing weight as it stretched out into the troop compartment, "…take…us…up!"

Nearly one-hundred meters away the Midcraft burst vertically out of the ocean's depths to evade the Trident and rotated around and shot south as it was bombarded by a hail of ballistic and missile fire from two of the nearest frigates and one missile destroyer, guided by a third-generation closed-network tactical weapons artificial intelligence system coordinating the attack between the ships. The high target strike rate, despite the Midcraft's speed and maneuverability, temporarily disabled the craft's shielding system, causing it to become plainly visible to radar and orbiting satellites almost instantaneously.

The platoon commander, seeing the alien craft under heavy attack as the CH-47 finally freed itself from the ocean's grip, deeply inhaled and shouted at it with all his might, "Eat shit motherfucker!"

Receiving the real-time tactical feed from one of the satellites, Admiral Bulheign aboard the new class of battleship named the USS Anvil, turned toward the weapons officer and ordered, "Screen fire six Shivs on that target!"

The *Shiv* was the name of a new nuclear shape-charged shell nearly 1,400 pounds in weight, fabricated specifically for the composite, non-ferrous sixteen-inch guns of the battleship. But what makes the Shiv unique from other nuclear tipped ballistic rounds, aside from the deployable guidance fins of the shell, is it was designed to channel the destructive power of a micro-nuclear explosion through a sleeve cone of depleted uranium surrounded by a casing of the most powerful neodymium. While the entire shell is vaporized by the explosion its conical shape, for those few milliseconds, is able to guide that raging power like a shaped charge, to penetrate and release most of the kinetic energy inside the target.

Within seconds the automated loading platforms chambered six Shiv shells into the massive sixteen-inch guns on the deck of the battleship and the targeting system rapidly turned the two giant turrets in the direction of the Midcraft that was still out of visual range and fired, rocking the mighty ship backward several feet in the ocean. Already at terminal velocity by the time the shells exited the barrels, the targeting system spread the shells using their fins to maximize the probability of impact and guided them to the target.

But just before impact the Midcraft vanished from the targeting computer's tracking system. Still, one of the Shivs successfully slammed into the alien craft, detonating the shell and unleashing its destructive power, having breeched the shield, consuming the entire craft inside the shield with the greatest effect damaging exposed engine conduits, related systems and vaporizing many of the exotic alloy hull plates built to withstand some of the deadliest radiation streams found in space. For almost an entire nautical mile, with the shield system destroyed, the craft shed portions of itself while it tumbled and veered at the mercy of airflows and the pilot's efforts to restabilize flight and restore the operation of critical systems. Though severely damaged, the Midcraft limped further southeast until the pilot was able to restore the distortion bubble and get them back on course to origin base.

Over the course of the next seven hours with crippled propulsion, they traveled northwest to the venting stratovolcano Mount Veniaminof, largely covered by a glacier, located in the Aleutian Range south of the waters of Bristol Bay. On its north-eastern side the pilot guided the craft into a gaping crevice for some seventy meters before veering sharply south into an artificial domed causeway that connected to the origin base the Serpqhtaq had erected when they originally arrived on Earth prior to first contact with the Archgen. It had purposefully been constructed deep within lava flows to shield it from detection by their adversaries, when the mighty glaciers were just beginning to stretch into the region.

Chapter Eight

"Congratulations, Mr. President!" one of several staffers cheered inside the oval office. A few others smiled warmly toward him while raising their fruit punch filled glasses.

After grabbing a glass for himself from the oval coffee table in front of his desk the President, a persuasive political maverick now sixty-three years old, raised his glass toward them with a smile, "Couldn't have done it without you all."

Leslie Wiezstrong, Chief of Staff and a political veteran stretching back decades in both the House of Representatives and Senate since her initial internship, pivoted in the direction of the staffers while taking a small sip from her own glass. In her early forties with long, wavy fiery red hair reaching to her waist, she wore a pink two-piece business knee-high adjustable strap dress with a long-sleeved blazer and matching closed round-toe, ankle strapped low-heel shoes. Her connections alone, through the halls of power, had shored up nearly twenty percent of the support needed for the *Humanity Act* to pass.

One of the purposes of the Humanity Act, given the increasing pace with which humans across all occupations were being replaced by artificial intelligence with no comparable wage alternatives, was to help ensure societal stability and that the tax revenue stream of the government persisted without, what had been forecasted - a collapse in the consumer-based economy and tax receipts, severe contraction of programs and investments, inability to guarantee safe trade routes and national interests, geo-political destabilization and an over-burdening of social systems like welfare that would assuredly balloon and bankrupt the nation leading to its dissolution and cannibalization by both nation-states and worldwide corporate behemoths beyond the regulatory reach of most others. The more significant purpose was to keep humans cognitively active, competitive, and to pursue life with the self-deterministic beliefs that had set the country apart from all the others – that each had the opportunity to shape their own destiny by their own hand.

The architects of the Humanity Act had envisioned the inevitable entropy, cognitive decline and even backwardation of the human race when their very existence, bound solely to a wage for profitable economic output from which they paid to live and perpetuate society, could not be realistically reduced to nothing more than the cost of mass-produced electricity. In comparison to the new generation of cognitive artificial intelligence, able to perform every task a human could perform from cleaning hotels to managing all logistics of a business and even making all more generalized strategic decisions guiding the direction of a business and even country, was able to procreate itself at dedicated assembly facilities in physical form exactly as designed and instantly trained within hours instead of almost a year of gestation for humans. As well, it did not require decades of resource expenditure, education, foodstuffs, housing and did not replicate any consumer spending patterns that a human would, nor even collect a wage…instead the only persistent pseudo-wage for AI to function – or be productive in business speak – was little more than the cost of electricity. While the architects had given consideration as to what business model could possibly endure in an environment where that business no longer had to relinquish any profit to humans to ensure its own survival, and thereby never perpetuate a resource intensive biologically-driven society via the wage mechanism, they realized that nation-states, the stewards of societal stability and order, would be forced to.

Yet the architects also realized that if the human race were to exist in the cosmos they would, at some point or another, encounter another race they may be forced to be competitive with. Ergo, the human race would need the resources, readily available, to find competitive advantage. It meant the sheer breadth of AI's access to gargantuan data sets and its decision-making speed, making even an army of human savants pale in comparison, could not be sidelined. It meant, for humans to persist into the future, they would still require a wage and from that also perpetuate society. It also meant humans had to be trained and immersed in specializations that organizations, for reasons of "market forces", would otherwise hand-off entirely to AI. That training was intended to prevent AI from becoming the only keeper of knowledge and the single force that all organizations would surrender themselves to, given time, reducing the human race into a state of perpetual subservience…and in a world where those very organizations would no longer exist – or at least not under human control.

The Act itself consisted of a few different sections meant to support commercial interests whom supported humanity. The first section was the *50 Rule*. The simplest section, it provided a certification and range of benefits by attesting that at least fifty percent of the labor force was human with no single department being one-hundred percent non-human. In exchange the commercial interest agreed to periodic audits for federal verification and re-certification.

The second section was the *30/70 Botshare*. This was also an auditable certification for comparable benefits but stipulated that just thirty-percent of the labor force was required to be human and the remaining seventy-percent could be AI but with the caveat being the AI being leveraged was from a Botshare either owned by the government or from government-certified third-party. The Botshare, under the government's regulatory eye, tracks the compute or each unit of "work" performed by the AI, or physical labor "work" performed by a physical robot driven with AI, and converts that into equivalent hours worked by a human, and sent through an industry-specific algorithms and, via a range of metrics maintained by the government such as product or service demand, pre-AI market driven automation and efficiency gains patterns impacting all occupational "work" which reduces the "wage" to "work" relationship year-over-year, converted into a dollar amount. With each Botshare representing a group of human-only stakeholders selected by application, that amount is paid by the commercial interest and evenly divided to the stakeholders which, naturally, becomes economic fuel and taxable income

The third section was the *Venture*. While this did not have a certification process, as it was meant to offer a very limited number of benefits for commercial interests whom did not participate in section one or two, it still had an audit requirement for validation purposes. That said, participants in the prior sections could also take advantage of the *Venture* section. In exchange for commercial interests putting dollars into Venture, spearheaded by the government to get humans off-world by establishing *Seed Outposts* (simple outposts supporting basic human biological needs, temporary habitat, commercial equipment staging and communication), benefits included relaxed off-world lease terms and the like.

Unlike the first three sections of the Act, the fourth section focuses on the government trades initiative supporting citizens with the newly formed *Petiole Foundation.* The foundation's primary mission is to support human off-world settlement and to that end, oversee and stimulate activities like mining, construction and manufacturing that would be involved but with minimal application of AI. In line with the intent of the Act, the foundation would employ citizens, most likely those already permanently displaced by AI in their occupations. However, given some of the benefits only a sovereign could offer, which will be detailed shortly, those not yet displaced could also be accepted. Ultimately all members of the foundation would be assessed for placement, trained over time and be bound to renewable labor contracts anywhere from three to seven years in duration. Once a contract is entered the member, along with any immediate family members, would be relocated to a small fortifiable town known as a *Burg* that could be best thought of as a largely self-sufficient military base without the rigid boundary, or the iron-hand of military order, precision and presentation; in the continental United States hundreds of them were established from existing towns with minimum existing infrastructure to support law enforcement, a hospital, a school and some degree of economic exchange such as a grocery store, consumer goods and the like to encourage human attachment, and thus future contract renewal. That said, Burgs were also established in territories of the United States. The reason for such a large geographic placement of Burgs was to ensure operational resilience and, at the same time, serve as the public face for the initiative with the broader populace. Lastly, should something happen in or near a Burg requiring evacuation, the entire town could be moved with logistical precision of the members to their new destination and roles.

All members, due to federal oversight, were bound to having all legal matters handled through a remote federal court, even for matters of state, and streamed with the local courthouse. That aside, the rest of a member's existence was normal just like everyone else except for the benefits. Modeled similar to the military, a Burg has at least one cafeteria and members could use that resource to get three free meals per day and per immediate family member through the use of a hand print. Additionally, members have free use of doctors and operations at the hospital as well as schools. In terms of housing, a member would be initially issued a rent-free house sufficient for the member and any immediate family. Then, at their contract renewal period, they could elect to buy or lease to own the property, or remain as a non-paying occupant. The reason one might choose the latter is, as a member accumulates years of service, those years can be used to be issued a different housing property to move to that may offer greater square footage or other amenities the current does not. But perhaps the most coveted benefit for newer members who submit their candidacy, is entrance into the yearly *Stellar Plot* drawing held at each Burg. The randomly selected member from the drawing is titled a terrestrial plot on a stellar planet or moon either near or at a location the government has interest in developing or has already developed and is seeking to strengthen. After title issuance the member then has the ability to transfer to a development there or be among the members who would establish a permanent presence, or, hold and do nothing until some point in the future. For more seasoned members with accumulated years of service, they could use those years to purchase title to a stellar plot themselves or, for those with no interest in living off-world, gift their years of service to another member. But, regardless of drawing or years of service, the geographic size of the stellar plot remains static and a member can only be titled one stellar plot.

After placing her free hand beneath the glass, Leslie turned toward the President, "I agree. The Humanity Act will not only shape our country but civilization itself."

The President considered it for a moment and admitted, "I don't know about all that, Leslie, but it will keep humans…you and I…as doers of a brighter future instead of passengers."

Leslie appreciated his humility even now. Having been in his orbit for several years, his genuine expression of it energized her resolve to support him every time she experienced it. "No question, sir. It is one thing to spend money and time to be educated by an AI and acquire an M.B.A. or an engineering degree. But at the end of the day, if AI is taking the lion's share of all those jobs, there is no impetus for people to even try. At least your Act keeps the door open so they can follow such pursuits with confidence. And have money to get there."

"That is my hope. And with Venture, help offset our costs with getting civilian outposts setup for the rest of it."

Leslie glanced around, trying to think of what he was referencing and then it donned on her, "Oh. You mean the Magnum Ambit, Stellar bonds and all that?"

The President took a drink and nodded.

Leslie lowered her hand and swirled the punch in her glass while thinking more about it, before she looked up at the President and said, with an excited expression, "You know?! I think I'm actually going to buy some Stellar land bonds on Mars. Make it my retirement home."

"I would totally visit, Leslie." the President smiled warmly after he placed his glass on the desk, "And we could enjoy some American Preference according to the 1922 U.S.P.C.C. rules. With, of course, my own piquet deck."

Hearing a familiar voice behind her, Leslie glanced at her wrist-watch before turning toward the Vice-

President and Secretary of Defense who were talking as they approached, "Time for our meeting already?"

They stopped next to her and the Vice-President jested, "Not quite yet. Figured we could crash your little party and get a free drink."

"Get one, gentlemen." the President urged, gesturing toward the coffee table.

As they did so, Leslie turned toward the Staffers and said, "Time to go. We have a meeting already I'm afraid."

Then, following behind the small gathering and closing the door behind them, she turned about and strode toward the three men while saying, "What do you say we settle in here and get to business?"

"Can't argue with that." the Secretary of Defense agreed, sitting in one of the cushioned chairs by the table.

Shortly thereafter the others followed suite, less the President who chose to sit on the edge of the desk, Leslie withdrew a compact tablet with attached stylus, approximately the size of a large smart phone and began scrolling, "So…what do we have for this slot…let's see."

"Mr. President." the Secretary of Defense opened, "I do have one matter which has not been scheduled."

Leslie stopped for a second to look up toward them.

"If I may, Leslie." the Secretary of Defense said politely.

Leslie, though mildly annoyed, darted her eyes over to him, "Well. Go ahead Vonch. Just don't hijack this meeting."

"You have my word." Then, shifting to the President he continued, "Undoubtedly, you have been getting briefings from General Lowinsky, so you are aware of the Serpqhtaq."

"Yes."

After repositioning himself in the chair, Vonch said, "A snap fleet was assembled under *mist order* to protect a commercial ship the…Sága. It was attacked by an underwater alien ship."

A mist order, which all officers had been trained on, was an order to conduct an official action but on unofficial grounds. In most situations involving such an order, officers would brief their crew under one of many labels that could be used without consequence in the event they were forced into questioning such as 'search and rescue' or 'training'.

"And how did our fine navy do?" the President asked, under the impression they would have the same success as had been seen with the alien base, "They stomp all over those scumbags?"

Curious herself, Leslie looked up from the tablet.

"The fleet's tactical weapons AI network scored a ninety-seven percent hit rate on the alien ship but our new battleship inflicted the most damage with its huge guns and one of those Shiv shells." Vonch articulated, holding off on the bad news, "Who would have thought they could be used to hit something in the air at those speeds."

"I knew our navy boys could get the job done!" the President said radiantly, hitting the top of the desk with his palm.

"Yes, sir." Vonch joined but then admitted, "The last reports we have indicate the alien ship was badly damaged. But we just didn't inflict enough to get past all their tech and bring it down. We lost tracking of it about forty-five nautical miles to the southwest."

"That is too bad, Vonch." the President grumbled in anger, looking down toward his shoes and the carpeted floor, "I would have liked an alien souvenir to put in a museum. You know something to tell to the world that this was our first victory – to come and take a look at our weak enemy."

"Me, too." the Vice President concurred.

Vonch looked between them and, after pressing his lips together, said, "We also lost the Sága. It was sunk by the alien attack. Dive and recovery operations will be starting any moment now for any survivors and to see what can be salvaged and demo'd."

"The Sága?" the President whispered heavily, lifting his head to look at Vonch in defeat, "That ship. The AI on-board was our ace against the aliens. Jesus, Vonch."

The air of uncomfortable silence filled the room with the President placing part of his weight on his palms upon the desk as he looked between them and then to the glasses on the coffee table, irritated with the notion that despite some of the navy's latest advances, they were still ill-equipped to face off against a single alien ship.

Leslie, shocked by the news, restrained herself from bringing up the next point of business for a few moments, given the President's disappointment. She did not know much about the true significance of the Sága or the AI but she did know how to read people and the interplay with bigger picture issues.

After sighing deeply, the President broke the silence and asked, "Is *Sky Jump*, at least, still feasible for us?"

Eager to change the subject and move on, Vonch replied, "It is, Mr. President. That is an ace we still have and would be impossible for those aliens to destroy."

The President looked squarely at Vonch, "I sincerely hope so, Secdef. We don't have many aces left."

Seeing her opportunity to get into the conversation, Leslie tapped on the tablet a few times and said, "Speaking of aces…for our meeting. Sir, now that we know the cause of all those huge fires and plans for Sky Jump I think we need to put something on the wire to let citizens know we are taking care of it. And galvanize support."

"You think that is wise, so soon after that tragedy?" the President asked while resting his elbows on his legs.

"Well, sir." Leslie started as she made some selections on her tablet and then pointed toward the large flat panel screen anchored on the west wall of the room, just above the artificial fireplace, "I think the secret is officially out…without being officially out."

The screen showed the amateur video footage of the Moon and the drifting overlay of the streamer as she pointed towards different areas of the video, on top of zooming and contracting actions of that footage, focusing on kinetic weapon discharges as well as some grainy footage of the SSHC cruisers' movements. While the footage lacked the resolution to expose the fighters themselves and the Serpqhtaq craft, Leslie froze the video when the gigantic Cruhapl appeared not far away.

"Ah." Vonch brushed off, "That's just one person out there. Anybody can make that sort of video nowadays."

"Many others, some from observatories in other countries, have started popping up as well." Leslie countered, "I think we should get ahead of it while its early. Get control and shape the narrative before someone else does. And, if this goes like I think it will, get support and volunteers if all that mess makes it down here."

Vonch frowned, disappointed by her lack of confidence and said, "It won't. If you have seen what has been put together…"

Leslie shot up and raised her hand, holding the tablet, at the screen and almost shouted, "That is already on our doorstep and we can't protect every square foot of Earth! Things will slip through and then it will be game on."

The President tapped his fingers against the desk before standing and then slowly walked around it toward his chair saying, "I'd prefer to play this safe. With our civilian expansion into the Solar System its inevitable they will come across something. Best to be in front of this early as an official source so we have credibility and trust capital to leverage when something pops up downstream. So, why don't you put together a speech for a video message about our overall plan to tango with the aliens hitting us below the belt?"

Leslie lowered her hand to consider it. Then she suggested, "How about a live *snap address* with our local supporters for national broadcast?"

"That's a good idea." the President agreed, sitting down and turning the chair to face them, "We should be able to rustle up enough people to fill the state room."

Leslie turned her head from side to side, "No. For something this big, we need a big audience. Like stadium big."

"Twenty thousand people? We'll need days…probably a week to get that type of turn out especially with all the chaos out there." the Vice President challenged.

"You think we'll need to hire busloads of actors to fill the seats that fast? With some of our training exercises we tap crisis actor firms. Shouldn't take long to mobilize." Vonch volunteered.

"Are you crazy?" Leslie moaned, "Look. We have marketing material right there. Get that carried on the networks with mention of the stadium snap address and I'm telling you; the stadium will fill itself in hours."

The Vice President turned his head toward the President, "I think that would work, sir. It's going to come down to the speech."

Leslie placed her hands on her hips and eyed the Vice President before shifting her focus to the President.

"Well," the President said as he rested his elbows on the desk and cupped his hands, "what are you waiting for, Leslie? Make it happen."

Leslie grinned and winked at the Vice President before she hurriedly left the room while saying, "Yes, Mr. President. One speech of a lifetime coming up!"

Vonch grinned to himself and drank from his glass.

"Anything else?"

Vonch pulled the glass away from his mouth and shook his head, darting his eyes toward the Vice President.

"No sir." the Vice President said.

The President raised his eyebrows and slid back in the chair, focused on the Vice President, "Great. Then I've got something for you."

The Vice President straightened himself in the chair, confident he could speak on any matter that the administration was involved with, "Okay. Let's have it."

"How is our *Wishing Well* program coming along?" the President questioned.

The Wishing Well program is the outgrowth of an old endeavor, now a few decades old, that had been started by an earlier administration. Due to the initial costs absorbed by the military to setup ore refiners in space to support military specific objectives, that administration expanded those objectives to include ore refinement and storage of precious metals for monetary purposes with the long-term vision of offering the ultimate off-world storage solution to other sovereigns with the vision that the metals could also be used to support economies and commerce both on and off-planet while ratcheting down hostilities for dwindling supplies of metals that had previously only been mined on the planet. But rather than having those sovereigns rocket their precious metals for vaulting in space, they would buy the refined metals mined in space and shuttled to two *Armoire Sites* under guard of the military. The extra cost associated with those sites, the fact that they could not be used to support military operations, and the reality that the military would, as the only force capable, be required to defend them, forced that administration to seek funding elsewhere. Following nearly a year of discussions, and transferring several interests the country had with Antarctica, a deal was reached with one ally and two aristocracies interested in breaking out of the growing number of scarcity deadlocks across the Earth and move into the vast, unutilized virgin spacescape. After the sites were established and metals ownership recorded by various means, it was not until decades later that those records and all future transactions would be recorded on the blockchain known as *Pistis*, a record system only accessible to participating sovereigns and managed by a neutral international unincorporated non-profit sovereign fiduciary structure they had established called *Eunomia,* following strict and enforceable measures participating sovereigns had drafted and bound themselves to.

Each Armoire Site is located in a space-gapped section of a rotating *Sector Hub* and each of those is located on the north and south cardinal points of the Sun, as viewed from the top of the solar system looking down; the east and west Sector Hubs are still being constructed but all are named according to their cardinal point such as North Sector Hub. Each Sector Hubs is located 284,000 km above the ecliptic and 1.7 AU from the Sun so that they are close to the asteroid belt and inner planets to provide consistent locations that ships going from one planet or asteroid to another can dock with. Their function is to provide a consistent point in space with which ships can refuel, restock, and otherwise conduct commerce before proceeding to their final destination and, with the exception of a military post and staff to support its operation, has no permanent residents. While more of a term used to convey travel to or from a Sector Hub, a *Radiant Route* is the flight path a ship follows, after relaying to a Sector Hub, to or from a hub so they can be monitored and a response ship launched if a critical issue surfaces. Since the Sector Hubs do not rotate around the Sun like the planets do and are stationed above them, the term also helps to clarify that the flight path will be a trajectory above the ecliptic instead of, in such cases as from Earth to Mars, largely along the ecliptic and a much larger distance.

"There are preliminary talks with Eunomia and another country who has expressed the desire to be brought on board to acquire gold and vault off world, with a high ratio to back off-world commercial endeavors. From what I understand so they can keep it isolated from terrestrial concerns. At least for the moment."

"Good. And, what about…" the President began, straining to recall the exact name of the new zero-gravity refining platform, "the Voltas?"

"The *Volta Sieves*?" the Vice President volunteered, assuming that was what the President meant.

"Yes." the President smiled, waving his hand in the air as if to dismiss the term, "I can't seem to remember the names of all that fancy equipment they use up there. I just know that one is good for money."

The Vice President chuckled lightly, "Yes, it is Mr. President. Well, as you know, refining gold is pretty simple to do because of its properties so we've always been able to achieve 99.9 percent purity at space mine sites. The problem has been on-site extraction and refining for silver."

After placing his glass on the coffee table he continued, "Well, the newly developed no-gravity electrolytic centrifugal smelting and refining cubes…Volta Sieves…permit silver to now be refined to 99.9 percent purity at each mining site. So, the only thing we actually need to shuttle for storage now is both vault and industrial use ready."

"It creates silver bars at the mine site?" Vonch asked with great curiosity.

The Vice President nodded, "Yes. It can also do the same for gold but that's always been easy for them to handle so I don't imagine they would be doing much gold refining with it. We could also move it from one mine to another with relative ease since it is the size of a refrigerator…without the refuse collectors."

"What kind of refined silver output are we talking here?"

"That sort of depends on the mine." the Vice President admitted, "By Eunomia statute, since silver is an industrial use metal, eighty percent of it must be sold to industry and twenty percent vaulted. During the last quarter at one of the larger off-world mines, a Volta Sieve refined 1.3 tons of silver into bars with 520 pounds to be vaulted."

"Impressive." the President exhaled with moderate satisfaction, "It really looks like we'll be able to make civilian life in space real."

“Here’s to that.” Vonch said while raising his glass toward him, “Doers, Mr. President.”

“Doers.” the President repeated while raising his own glass.

Chapter Nine

General Lowinsky waited patiently in the corridor for Mac and Jacob to finish leaving the gifts they had gotten for their wives and to come to terms with their gradually improving conditions. Lionak slowly paced nearby.

Once the door opened, Mac and Jacob exited the room followed by Doctor Fruitz who had been watching them like a hawk to ensure they did not compromise the well-being of her patients.

“General. Didn’t expect to see you here.” Jacob said, surprised to see him in the corridor.

“Well, just finished a marathon of meetings and needed to walk around.” the general replied as he lifted his hands in the air, “So I thought I’d take a stroll here and meet up with you guys.”

The doctor casually touched Jacob’s arm as she passed between them on her way to the C.T.C. room, “Please give me a second. I’ve got to check on something.”

“Your wives are okay?” Lionak asked in a solemn tone of voice.

Both of them said ‘Yes’ and Jacob elaborated a bit further, “The doctor showed us how to read some of the equipment and they are doing okay. Even improving.”

“Yeah,” Mac joined, “I think she called the healing machines a Medicra.”

Jacob nodded.

“That is great news.” Lionak smiled.

"So…what of Zorin?" Jacob asked in return, "Can't say I would be happy with being down in the basement. In a smoky box."

Lionak adjusted his sleeve to buy him a few moments before he finally spoke, "The same from what I can tell."

Mac rolled his lips into a grin of weak optimism and grasped Lionak's shoulder, "He'll make it, you'll see."

"The healing machines around here are the best I've ever seen." Jacob reinforced with positivity even though he had never heard of them before.

"I'll make sure of it." the general added, though part of him was drawn to assessing the capabilities of the dragon and how that might be used to strengthen the military. And, to do that, a live subject was preferable to a dead one.

Exiting the room with Spewge collared and connected to a short leash, the doctor strained against the dog as he forced his way toward Jacob, "This patient is ready to be signed-out!"

"Spewge!" Jacob exclaimed as the large dog came to his side and restlessly strutted around.

Seeing the doctor struggle Jacob collected himself and, while pointing down toward the dog, commanded, "Stop! Sit!"

The dog promptly sat, his eyes eagerly moving back and forth from Jacob to the others, muscles flexing in anticipation of bolting in some random direction at a moment's notice.

The doctor happily handed the leash to Jacob and lightly exhaled, "That's better exercise than running around base!"

"You're telling me, doc. Sure keeps that spare tire away." Jacob responded while grabbing his abdomen before he knelt down and wrapped an arm around the dog.

"Well. Gentlemen." the general said as he maneuvered to face the small crowd, "Shall we continue to our next destination?"

"Next destination?" Mac mumbled.

Jacob stood up and looked between them, oblivious as to what the general was referring to.

"Yes, sir. Operation Javelin."

"Never heard of it." Jacob said plainly while regripping the leash.

"It is the official op to neutralize the alien colonization fleet." the general specified.

"Since you put it like that, let's go!" Mac urged, more than ready to dish out some punishment for the firestorms and what had been done to his wife.

"Hold on now." Jacob frowned, raising his free hand, "Before I go anywhere, I've got to get my kids."

"Jacob." the general said sternly, "They have been secured and are in-route as we speak."

"You have them?"

General Lowinsky gripped his waist belt and said, "I have them under armed escort, Jacob."

Jacob eyed the general for a split second and then the others as he weighed the situation. After looking back toward the room with his wife, now in a safe location, he sighed, "Then…I am ready, sir."

"And you?" the general asked in Lionak's direction.

"I've got my staff and the White Magic." Lionak rumbled, thinking of what happened to Chief Zorin, "Not even a Death Raiden will stop me."

The general, unfamiliar with what Lionak spoke of, guessed it meant he was ready and ordered, "Follow me."

A few hours later, aboard the SR-95, they arrived at Fort Defiant, the only remaining operational Earth based site constructing large ships and equipment for the space fleet since most of those activities were transitioning to now take place off-world. The Fort also has the unique qualification of being the first base to construct and launch dozens of the heavy rockets used to establish continuous manned military presence in space. Located within

Maverick Mountain, situated northeast of Wilcox Dry Lake found in the Southeast of Arizona, the weathered partial remains of the heavy rocket launch platform are still visible at bottom of Rough Canyon to the north. As an integral hub for other bases in a four-hundred-mile radius, an underground tunnel network connects the base to others from which personnel, equipment, material and some smaller spacecraft are transported, free of public discovery and scrutiny.

Slowing its descent, the pilot of the SR-95 skillfully maneuvered through a small concealed entrance near the bottom of Angle Canyon and sharply descended four-hundred-seventy meters before landing. As he powered down several systems, the general turned toward the others and said, "Welcome to Fort Defiant, our first and finest base for off-world excursions."

Once they exited the craft the general led them through the domed flight deck, dimly lit with red bulb lights lining the cracked concrete walls, to a guarded grey steel door nearly one and one-half feet thick with a simple round silver knob and two key-pass pads affixed to it. After the general presented himself to the guard nearest the door, together they pressed their pass cards on the key-pass pads and the four deadbolts locking the door in place retracted, releasing it.

Opening the door, the general turned toward them and said, "After you."

"Judging from the looks of this place, I guess the pilot was right. This does look like it could be the first." Mac commented as he scanned around himself noting, among other things, the old lighting system in the flight deck and the sets of double bulb light fixtures spaced overhead, containing a red bulb and a white bulb, the latter of which was illuminated making the fourteen-foot-wide corridor brighter than what one would expect for their size.

"She's old but strong." the general grinned, leading them down the corridor to a key-pass pad protected supply room. After he presented his pass card and pulled the door open while gesturing for them to enter, he added, "The outer walls are made of three four-foot-thick reinforced concrete walls, each separated by five inches of ballistic steel plate. If you wanted to ride out the end of the world, it would be here if you could not get to the Moon C.O.G. complex."

After everyone entered the supply room measuring eight meters cubed and loaded with sturdy racks packed with crates and boxes, the general located and opened a box labeled 'Fleet Uniforms – Ruby' and opened it. Having estimated their sizes, he pulled out a stiff black ballcap and flight suite with two embroidered patches, the left shoulder bearing a grey-colored thick lightning bolt and a red-colored javelin in its center with a red-colored ruby beneath it, and the right shoulder bearing the grey-colored Winged Lion insignia painted onto ships of the space fleet. He handed it to Jacob. Then he did the same for Mac and Lionak.

"What is this for?" Lionak asked, reluctantly accepting the uniform.

"I need you to put that on and put your clothes in this locker here." General Lowinsky said as he pointed to an empty locker with a key-pass pad and his name and rank stenciled on it in yellow, near the room's door, "I'll return them when our op is over."

Being the first to slip on the uniform, Jacob walked over to the locker and opened it. Surprised that it was empty, he placed his clothes and shoes in it and said, "You don't use this, general?"

The general looked over at the locker as he approached a different box on one of the racks, "Never had a need for it. I'm not even sure I have any civilian clothes or effects to put in there."

"Hard core." Mac whispered to himself as he zipped up the uniform, mentally visualizing the general's closet being filled with nothing more than camouflage fatigues, boots and a dress uniform.

Opening the box and finding black, mid-shin high boots with velcro straps, the general hit the box a few times and said, "Get your footwear here."

Once everyone had changed and placed their belongings in the locker, the general closed it and activated the double-lock mechanism by pressing his pass card on the pad.

"Are we going to get one of those cards, too?" Jacob asked, realizing he did not have one for the base.

Leading them out of the room and straight through a corridor intersection to a heavy steel gate that filled the entire width of the corridor, the general stopped next to a key-pass pad and said, "Where you guys are going, you won't need these cards."

"We won't?" Mac said questioningly, uneasy with the idea of not having a card while being in the middle of a base where every door seemed to require one.

The general closed his eyes momentarily and turned his head from side to side.

"If I might ask, general, where are we going?" Jacob asked, looking between them.

Pressing the pass card on the pad bolted to the wall of the corridor, causing the heavy gate to slowly retract into the ceiling, the general casually said, "Sky Jump."

Once the gate stopped the general proceeded, followed by the others, into the colossal construction and repair dry-dock that had been built in the mountain. Measuring five-hundred meters in length by three-hundred meters in width and one-hundred meters in height at the perimeter arching to three-hundred-seventy-meters toward the center, the floor space alone was large enough to accommodate over thirty football fields.

"Holy shit." Jacob muttered, taken aback by the vast open space and the occasional large rebar-wrapped column supporting the metal-skinned ceiling.

"Wow." Mac grunted, amazed that such a large structure had been built inside the mountain, "How many contractors do you have working in here to keep all this going?"

General Lowinsky cupped his hand toward Mac and said, "Zero. For something like this, we use compartmentalized front projects far removed from here where contractors may be tapped to solve a particular issue one of our Ruby engineering teams may be having."

"Ruby?" Mac repeated.

The general slowed his pace somewhat to come alongside Mac as he looked at him and clarified, "The patch on your shoulder bears the Ruby symbol. That denotes Ruby clearance reserved for missions so critical that they are beyond classification. Beyond classification means that not even the highest-ranked military personnel with the highest classification clearance can access anything about such missions without Ruby clearance. And definitely not civilian personnel."

"You're talking about black projects." Jacob said.

"Beyond black actually." the general smirked.

"The Ruby engineering teams, then, basically design, prototype and build all the really cool tech like these ships?" Jacob wondered.

"Yes."

Turning to his left and walking behind one of the new Wolf-class heavy cruisers finishing construction the general pointed at it and said, "That is our new class of heavy cruiser, the SSHC-30…an upgrade of the SSHC-20."

"Holy shit to that, too." Mac gawked, looking ahead of them to see three others, each resting on a wheeled flat-bed trailer of some type, "That's what, a couple hundred feet long?"

As the general continued walking past another SSHC-30 and some soldiers gathered around a work bench, he turned slightly toward them and said, "365 meters in length by about 31 meters in height. Each can field twenty-six SSB fighters…and they have a few extra offensive systems to wreak havoc from a distance."

Mac's eyes widened at the numbers, "So these are aircraft carriers for space."

"Yes." the general nodded.

"Without the flat top." Jacob said, observing their shape.

Peering beyond the fourth, Jacob spotted the stern of another ship in the distance with a different profile, "And that down there?"

Turning to his right, between two of the cruisers into a space resembling an open but narrow runway, the general proudly said, "One of our battleships. A rather nasty monstrosity at that."

"And it has fighters, too?" Lionak asked, dodging three soldiers wearing flight suits matching his as they walked past.

"No." the general responded.

"Hey what about those people over there?" Mac said, gesturing toward three people, one of which setting up a camera on a tripod, clothed in civilian attire, "They have Ruby clearance?"

The general looked over at them and said, "They do. Everyone here does. We have Ruby clearance personnel in many different occupations to interface with the civilian world and to ensure missions are not compromised. In their case, to film a segment on these ships for public awareness and branding."

Jacob frowned and said, "Taking video of the ships your teams assembled inside a mountain and putting it in the public is okay?"

The general looked briefly at Jacob, understanding where he was going, and said, "In this case it is. Besides, seeing these ships…which are the latest iteration of what has already been seen by the general population…does not divulge the technology hidden beneath their exterior. Technology that the military has exclusive knowledge and control over."

"Ah." Jacob nodded, "In part the filming is officially establishing that the ships they have seen are U.S. and not of some other country out there."

"Yes."

Continuing to take in the impressive-looking ships and activity around him, Mac posited, "So you build all space ships here."

"There was another decades ago when we were launching heavy rockets, but once that was no longer needed, it was re-purposed." the general recalled, "This is the last active base still building big ships for the space fleet."

As they reached the approximate center of the vast dry-dock, where the ceiling arched to its highest point, Jacob questioned, "Wouldn't it be better to build space ships in space? I mean, the amount of fuel required must be incalculable to get these into space."

General Lowinsky stopped and faced Jacob with an almost amused expression, "Unlike the heavy rockets of yore, these do not derive thrust from a liquid propellant."

The general placed a hand on his hip and waited for a moment in anticipation of the next question, or for someone to notice the significance of where they stood.

Mac, pointing at one of the long flat-bed trailers, assumed, "Then you wheel these out to a launch platform somewhere I am guessing."

"Well," the general acknowledged, glancing over one of the trailers, "we do wheel these around. But, just to position them where we are standing. Then the ships are rotated up to launch through that."

The general pointed above their heads toward two massive doors, collectively shaped like a hexagon, at the ceiling's highest point, similar in design to that of the Minuteman launcher closure door, with the exception that these open outwards.

After a few seconds the general added, "Now that we have the capacity, some ships have been built in space."

"Why are these not built there?" Lionak asked, looking back down toward the general.

"Many reasons, Lionak." the general said while he lowered his arm, "The most relevant is that these ships started construction several years ago when we did not quite have the build capacity that we now have in space."

"And you're going to launch them through that door up there to get them into space?" Mac surmised confidently.

"No." the general countered as he began walking forward again, "These are actually going through what we call the *Big Nut* to another dimension."

The Big Nut is the scaled-up version of the hexagonal torus prototype that Janus had a hand in constructing in the desert that replicated the magically created dimensional portal that had been cast when Chief Zorin was pursuing the Baron in this dimension. Together with the dish array to augment the torus's angled field emissions, provided the mechanical means to open dimensional portals without any proficiency in magic. The general, realizing the importance of securing the newly discovered dimension with large military hardware, had orchestrated the Big Nut's construction in parallel with the prototype. In doing so, not only could its existence be better masked in paper trails, but he would have the means to move the hardware required from deep within a base under military control.

"Big nut." Mac snickered to himself, his mind impulsively thinking of human biology, "Does it come with a bag or is that on the other side?"

Jacob wheeled toward Mac with a grin and added, "Teabag, hooah!"

Rather than answer the general just shook his head.

As they reached the opposite end of the dry-dock, and the hexagonal torus structure towering before them measuring seventy-five meters in diameter with its open center measuring forty-five meters, and the dish array beyond that, Jacob shifted his thought back to what the general had said and he still did not quite understand what the general meant.

Pointing at the structure Jacob said, "If you are sending all the ships through that Big Nut to the Realm, they will not make it to space here. The Realm is like a different world…maybe even universe."

Equally puzzled, both Lionak and Mac looked at the general for an explanation.

General Lowinsky stopped and admitted, "You are right. But if we were to launch our ships from here, they are not fast enough to intercept the alien fleet before it enters our Solar System…which is way too large for us to monitor, let alone defend if they were to scatter to asteroid belts or planets. The only realistic chance we have at this point is to hit them while they are clustered together by launching from here to the Realm as you call it."

Jacob shook his head from side to side and confessed, "I guess I just don't get it."

Just then, before the general could respond, a slight tremor rolled through the base loosening some pockets of earth that fell from the ceiling. Further away the clank of a metal tool echoed through the dry-dock followed shortly thereafter by a muffled, but loud, expletive.

"Best to see." the general said evenly after waiting for the tremor to pass, "That is why we are using this to go to Sky Jump."

"Sky Jump is in the Realm?" Mac questioned, knowing he had not seen any technologically advanced equipment or structures during his time there.

"It is."

The general motioned them toward a windowless tube-shaped transport, nicknamed the *Puddle Jumper*, with a single continuous sensor strip that wrapped around its exterior, a short ramp and two articulated liquid thruster legs joined near each end. The reason for the nickname was because all base personnel had been trained to fly it and the craft carried the minimum amount of liquid fuel required for seven minutes of flight time – just enough time to take-off, maneuver such as through a portal and land. That exceedingly short flight-time had been purposefully engineered into the transport primarily to prevent it from being used to fly beyond the perimeter of a base by personnel who were not pilots, among other considerations. To their credit the Ruby engineers, thinking from a combat point of view, had added a low-weight self-healing mechanism in the event the fuel tank inside the underbelly was punctured by weapons fire or from an accident. That mechanism was the encapsulation of a two-inch thick synthetic cellulose membrane liner around the tank itself. While puncturing the liner itself did nothing, if the tank was compromised and fuel or un-gassed vapor crossed into the liner, the membrane immediately around the puncture would react to the fuel, expand and then harden into an inert shell thereby resealing the tank and minimizing fuel loss.

After the general got to the top of the ramp he said, "Let's get aboard and be on our way."

Once everyone got aboard and the ramp retracted into the lower portion of the transport, the general closed the rear access door, walked through the isle of the eight-passenger seat cabin to the cockpit where the pilot was seated.

After sitting next to the pilot and clasping the seat belt, the general ordered, "Take us to Sky Jump."

"Yes sir!" the pilot acknowledged, promptly flipping some switches and signaling the control room to activate the portal.

Once it had been activated, the pilot grabbed the joystick before him with one hand while pulling a horizontal handle attached into a semi-circular guide channel to his left, causing the thrusters to come to life and force the transport into the air. Then, as the pilot moved the joystick, the thrusters articulated themselves accordingly by moving the transport in the air before the portal. After verifying the transport's position, the pilot pulled further back on the horizontal handle while pushing forward on the joystick causing the transport to lurch ahead into the portal and disappear from sight.

Chapter Ten

Having arrived at Sky Jump in the dead of night to the occasional gust of cool, choppy, air and absent moonlight, neither Jacob or Mac knew where they were although Lionak, linked to Metsys keep and feeling its White Magic, estimated they were no more than half-a-day's ride away. He had also felt the presence of a Guardian nearby and a powerful, continuous radiating of White Magic from beneath his feet.

The next morning, after collecting themselves, the trio exited the barracks-like quarters they had been escorted to and roamed through hallways in search of food. While the quarters contained five sleeping racks and full-sized closets as long as a rack, each set between them as to form a moveable privacy barrier, along with a separate walled bathroom consisting of a small sink, stand-up shower and a toilet, there was no refrigerator, food bin, or even a single box of MRE's.

"Nothing quite like the smell of cedar in the morning." Mac yawned, still able to detect the fragrance lingering in the air, released by the walls around them; thin wooden planks tightly joined, lining the hallways. The same planks were also used in the quarters.

The wood the planks were cut from had been identified by the autonomous cyborg known as Two during the resource acquisition phase of the base's construction meant to use natively available materials thereby minimizing considerable resource movement across dimensions and the probability of the base's discovery from such movement. The wood, cut from the *Dragon Skin Tree* and only found in a small mountainous region outside the Kingdom of Amagleituk, possessed incredible properties uniquely suited for the base and minimized the need for mining and complex metallurgical techniques required to create high-strength alloys commonly seen with ships of the fleet. That is, the wood with the weight and fibrous density of balsa wood, had the same strength characteristics as thin sheets of iron created through the process of taking molten iron and compressing it through a series of ceramic rollers containing intense magnetic fields to align the atoms into a uniform mesh pattern.

"Yeah," Jacob agreed, knocking on the wall a few times as they progressed, "this is the first time I've seen base barracks with wooden walls everywhere. Usually, they are painted concrete. Or cinder blocks or something."

Lionak glanced at the nearest wall but was unimpressed by their construction or the comparison. Moving slightly to avoid colliding with Spewge who had temporarily stopped for some unknown reason before bursting forth again, pressed, "You know where you are going, Jacob?"

"Me?" Jacob said as he reeled in some of the leash that Spewge was collared to, "No. But this base must have a chow hall somewhere. If they don't I say you teleport us to our great hall in the Guardian's stronghold. I know there's slop there."

"Humm. You know what." Mac said with an excited expression, the idea having just popped up in his mind, "We can actually go anywhere here with Lionak. Say to that tavern in the city?"

Jacob squinted his eyes at Mac for a moment, "Ah. You mean the one you met Regan at? Looking to reminisce?"

Mac blushed slightly at the idea, though that had not been his intent, and clarified, "Ah no. They have some fine drink and those turkey legs are just so good. Oh. My. God."

"Indeed." Lionak agreed, "Well what do you say? We roam around here like blindfolded rats or go where the cheese is?"

Jacob considered the offer as they crossed a few hallways, also wondering why base personnel wearing similar uniforms as his frowned at him while they passed. Then, in Mac's direction, he said, "Why am I getting the stink eye?"

Puzzled, Mac briefly looked behind them at one of the soldiers they had passed and then back, "I have no idea. Your fly is zipped, isn't it?"

Startled by the thought, Jacob snapped his eyes down to confirm everything is as it should be and then sighed, "Too early in the morning for that shit, Mac."

"Well?" Lionak pushed, eyeing Jacob and ready to summon his Staff.

Jacob, thinking of how they would inform the general and communication in a broader sense if they were to leave, grimaced, "I would love to but we'd have to find the general first, sign for a radio set and all that. I doubt he'd appreciate us just taking off without any way to contact us."

After turning right into another hallway with considerably more soldiers, an open archway twelve meters ahead to their left and the growing aroma of sausage, eggs, toast, other food and even a mix of different coffees, Mac victoriously declared, "Slop ahead!"

Mildly disappointed that they had stumbled across the chow hall, Lionak quietly exhaled but followed them into the large windowless eating area capable of spaciously seating one-hundred-and-twenty soldiers distributed among round tables, each with ten chairs assembled from aluminum legs and fairly rigid plastic seats.

Jacob, trailed by Mac and Lionak, grabbed a large tray to his right and then placed it on a long slide protruding from a ten-meter-long food table shielded with contoured plexiglass designed to protect the food from contamination by those in line. Then he reeled in more of the leash to prevent Spewge from entangling anyone.

Step by slow step they advanced, asking servers standing at regular intervals along the table for different items.

About midway through, Mac overheard one of the female servers say to another, "I'd like that carrot. Ummm!"

Not getting what she was referring to, Mac looked in the direction the server was fixated upon and happened to see a chiseled, athletically-built male in gym attire just as he was turning toward the archway after placing his tray in a collection bin, the act having pinched part of the long, baggy shorts as to highlight the shape of his buttocks.

The server's friend elbowed her and wondered, "Isn't he a medic? You should burn yourself on that toaster and get some one-on-one time. Get things taken care of. You smelling what I'm cooking? If you don't, I will!"

Mac grinned to himself and casually looked back pretending he didn't hear them banter back and forth.

After continuing forward and stopping in front of a selection of desserts and a stocky male server, Mac pointed and said, "I'll take that plain softie, please."

The server pointed at the small plate to confirm and then passed the plain glazed donut to Mac.

Then, just as he placed the small plate on his tray, a Vigilant 1 robot dog entered the chow hall, the same model that had been for sale in the retail consumer market. However, the units recently acquired by the military to eventually replace biological canines were repurposed for military police duty. And, although it had been repurposed in terms of the pre-trained model it used, it was still as autonomous and as realistic and fluid as the biological counterpart it had been designed after.

After stopping a few meters inside the chow hall to sweep the area, its ears and nose twitching to record sensor data several times more sensitive than a canine, it continued forward in search of anything considered a threat or danger to soldiers as well as the base.

Spotting a fellow dog, Spewge bound up and lurched toward the robot, causing Jacob to wheel around involuntarily before he regained his footing and forcefully pulled back on the leash, inadvertently bumping into a rather large and muscular soldier in line that was standing in front of him.

The towering soldier, nearly five inches taller than Jacob, turned to glare at him and roared, "The hell are you doing?! Your MUTT is not allowed on base!"

Conversations in the chow hall quieted down.

Not one to back down from such an aggressive stance and the demeaning overtone toward his dog, Jacob's jaw twitched and in a strong but balanced tone challenged, "We gonna cross dicks?!"

The soldier, after glancing over Jacob, confidently smiled and with animated eyes blasted back, "You got that right! I'm gonna strum these knuckles on your face like a guitar." Then, noticing the scowl from Mac, he added, "And your friend there, if he doesn't mind his business!"

Vigilant 1 slowly advanced toward them, focused on the behavior and movement of the two soldiers, minimally concerned with the muscular canine because dogs were more predictable and easily subdued with an immediate clasping attack to the throat just below the jaw whereas its training for subduing humans required completion of several escalatory submission techniques before it could attack the throat which could potentially kill the target.

Jacob, unphased by the intimidation, relaxed himself somewhat, prepared for kinetic action and forcefully taunted, "Guitar, what?! I don't speak freak…!"

But before he could finish his sentence an older, seasoned chef with the rank of chief petty officer burst into the chow hall from the adjoining food preparation space behind the food table, zeroed in on the hulking soldier and thundered, "Sergeant Sigg! Don't get me started again!"

In response to the interruption the sergeant made a tight fist causing the muscles of his forearm to bulge out, but then relaxed it as he turned his head toward the chef.

Locking eyes, the chief blared, "Are we on H.M.S. Fuckall, sergeant?! I'll come right over these softies and set your ass straight!"

Sergeant Sigg straightened himself, remembering what had happened last time, and forcefully exhaled. Then, in a more even tone of voice, said, "No chief…but he has a bio dog."

"I…!" the chief snapped before he raised his hand and nodded his head, "Just move out, sergeant."

With little hesitation the sergeant scooped up his tray, grabbed a bottled energy drink and temporarily glanced back at Jacob and Mac before he turned and walked toward a table.

Vigilant 1 retreated a few steps to keep the two soldiers in view as the sergeant strode off. Once he sat at a table, the robot scanned Spewge and then continued through the chow hall occasionally altering its path to observe each soldier until its situational conflict cool-down timer expired.

Placing his hands on his hips, the chief looked at Jacob, "He is right. Biological animals are not allowed in here, or Sky Jump in general."

Jacob nodded in acknowledgement even though he had not been aware of the rule and said, "It won't happen again chief."

"Good." the chief replied, "Since you already have your food, this one is on the house as long as you keep your dog under control. We square?"

"Square."

"Hooyah." the chief grunted before turning and walking back into the adjoining room, relieved he would not be filing disciplinary paperwork in addition to the work he still needed to get done.

After grabbing a bottled vitamin drink from a vertical dispensing rack at the end of the table, Mac turned and followed Jacob to a table as he said, "After that meet-and-greet, turns out I don't need coffee after all."

Spotting a table with enough open chairs for the three of them, Jacob placed his tray on it and then lashed the leash to the chair and sat down, joined thereafter by Mac and Lionak.

Shortly after they began eating a soldier sitting across the table from Jacob, who had been talking to another next to him, nodded at Jacob and with an uncommon accent said, "You got some nads dancing with that grizzly. That motherfucker ripped the head off a base sentry robot a while back with his bare hands. Little good that did when the robot didn't die and still restrained him."

One of the soldiers near him chuckled between bites.

"Wouldn't be the first time." Jacob responded, casually looking up from his tray toward the soldier with a slight grin, recalling his hand-to-hand fight with King Doron, leader of the barbarians, and his similarity to the sergeant.

The soldier's eyes briefly danced over Jacob before he glanced at Mac and Lionak and back in an attempt to gauge their combat experience. Then he smiled warmly and introduced himself, "Well, don't mind Sigg. He's quick to step in the shit. I'm Sergeant Waklopin by the way. Good to see new meat around here."

Jacob raised a balled fist across the table and, after the sergeant bumped it with his own, reciprocated, "Good to meet you. I am Staff Sergeant Quentin."

Sergeant Waklopin thought for a minute before he repeated, as to adjust his accent, "Kauintin…Quentinn. As in San Quentin?"

Jacob drank from his coffee cup and then shook his head slightly, mildly amused by the association he had not heard in several years, "I prefer more like the war-hardened town in Europe more than the prison."

"Ah. Okay." Sergeant Waklopin said while grabbing a partially consumed slice of toast, unaware of what Jacob was talking about, "Don't know much about that part of the world."

Jacob chuckled, "Naw, me neither, actually…just a few things here and there. But you can just call me Jacob."

On its return from sweeping the far end of the chow hall, Vigilant 1 stopped for a moment to scan Jacob to assess his aggression state before continuing toward the archway.

"Great then!" the sergeant responded, "So much simpler. I am Hoc! Even simpler."

Gesturing toward the others, Jacob said, "And this is Mac and Lionak."

While Mac acknowledged and bumped fists with the sergeant, Lionak was preoccupied with experiencing the unique taste of the softie he had gotten while overhearing the conversation of the two soldiers seated near the sergeant who were joking about their latest victim and the *Sweat Shot*.

"If you don't mind me asking, what is a sweat shot?" Lionak inquired curiously.

One of them looked over and proudly said, "A special concoction you can only brew in this dimension that we discovered consisting of whiskey and the strained juice of a native fire vine…sort of like a hot pepper."

"Really." Lionak mumbled, thinking as to what species of vine they were referring to. Then he volunteered, "The Xouplai vine?"

The soldier shrugged, "I think it was something like that."

"What does this brew do?"

The soldier looked at his friend for a second and in a much more serious tone, as if he had personally experienced it, admitted, "Each swig causes profuse, almost instant, sweating. We've never seen anyone make it to the third. Not even Sigg over there."

"That's it?" Lionak grunted, thinking of several botanical mixtures he could combine that would do much more than that, and without magic.

His friend frowned and confessed, "Bro. That's just the start. It is fire in AND out. No joke."

"Fire in and out?" Jacob repeated, having become interested in the conversation and the mysterious alcoholic mixture they had whipped up.

"Yeah. It's like drinking fire and then dropping a loaf – on fire." the friend detailed.

The soldier burst out laughing at the thought but his friend nudged him and lamented, "That shit's not funny! I had to put an ice-pack on my ass to put that shit out."

The soldier burst out laughing again.

The edge of Jacob's mouth curled up to form a partial smile before he shook his head and took another bite of his scrambled eggs that had been mixed with chopped onions, green peppers, tomatoes and cheese.

"Talk about torture." Mac mumbled between bites of herbed and slow-roasted chicken.

Lionak, due to the soldier's laughter, impulsively smiled before he caught himself and followed with another question, "How did you get your hands on that fire vine? I have seen no gardens or farm plots here."

"Ah yeah." the soldier's friend said, gently hitting the table with the tips of his fingers, "We get it brought here. The damn puddle jumpers don't have the range to get off base and return."

"You don't have horses here?"

"Horses?" the friend scoffed, mystified as to why Lionak would ask such an insane question, "Are you crazy?"

"Look." the soldier butted in, "Between us, we've been getting them in deliveries of food that the Guardians here take care of…you know, the dragons."

"The Silver Dragons?" Lionak questioned.

The soldier shook his head and swept his eyes between the newcomers as he said, "No. Our group made friends with some of them but the red ones are the ones that helped us. The silver ones were too uptight about adding extras to deliveries which I don't get. It's just a vine."

"At least they tolerate it." his friend noted.

"Yeah. True." the soldier confirmed.

After placing the cup on the tray, Jacob looked at the two and said, "How long has that been going on?"

The soldier leaned on the table with his forearms, thinking, and sighed, "Man. I'm not sure. Definitely before my first deployment though. Based on what was told to me, I want to say shortly after Sky Jump had been built and maybe the second deployment rotation of troops?"

"A while ago." his friend mumbled.

What none of them knew regarding the history around Sky Jump's construction was that Janus, following its instinct to maximize self-preservation and before it had negotiated a mutually beneficial arrangement with General Lowinsky, had altered the expeditionary team roster to include three cyborg units that were sent during John's second foray in the Realm to establish diplomatic, but secret, relations with the regional King and his alliance with the Guardians though that was unknown to both Janus and John at the time. While each cyborg had the task of guarding team members during their waking hours, each, because they didn't require sleep, had a different task when the team members slept. And, while the desert base's destruction shortly after the team had been sent and the emergence of the Arch-Demon in those same sands had not been anticipated, Janus had deduced that it would not be able to communicate with the cyborgs involved with Sky Jump when the dimensional portal was closed. Because of that significant limitation Janus had uploaded a large trained model to each cyborg unit, allowing them to function autonomously without direct oversight with the purpose of building Sky Jump with *Zero* trained in linguistics and diplomacy, *One* trained in equipment fabrication and *Two* trained in architectural construction. Then, following its completion, Janus had planned for the cyborgs to return in order to re-program them with a new model dedicated to extracting the artificial intelligence from the Sága and integrating its network into the base, free from the confines of the large and vulnerable ocean vessel. Even though the cyborgs were able to complete their assigned tasks following Zero's negotiation with the King, due to the base's destruction, they were unable to return for re-programming and were later deactivated and placed in specialized sustainment chambers aboard Sky Jump. It was not until General Lowinsky completed construction of the Big Nut, and following their agreement, that Janus would again have access to Sky Jump with the caveat of it falling under military protection and control.

After a short pause the soldier leaned in Jacob's direction, "Why do you ask? You looking to get something from this place?"

Jacob shook his head, "No. You don't have any idea just how one of us would know of the vine's existence in this dimension to know what to ask for?"

"No idea sarge."

Jacob stood and took his tray to the collection bin with a puzzled look. Once he returned, he unlashed the leash and sat down again, "Just seems kind of weird to me."

"Indeed." Lionak grunted, placing the last of the softie in his mouth.

"You're not going to snitch on us, are you?"

Jacob reared back a little and frowned, "Over a vine and some burning ass? Are you serious? No. Your party trick is safe with us."

"Check." the soldier beamed with relief. Shortly thereafter he rose, collected his tray and, along with his friend, moved toward the collection bin but stopped long enough to say, "Just gimme the word when you want to try a shot."

Jacob feigned a weak salute in return and turned toward Hoc, "You try that stuff, too?"

Hoc's eyebrows raised as he said, "No way! I'm not insane."

Jacob laughed to himself and said, "Me neither…last time I checked. You guys ready to find the general?"

Mac finished screwing the cap back on the bottle and stood, "Yeah."

"Speaking of brass," Hoc said, jerking his head in the direction of the archway, "a general just walked in."

Looking over, Jacob spotted the general and rose to his feet, adjusting the leash, "That's the one, Hoc. Later."

"Later sarge."

After crossing the room with Mac and Lionak, Jacob stopped before General Lowinsky and said, "We were just going to find you, sir. Should we come back when you've gotten something?"

"No." the general said as he pointed a thumb toward Phentities standing next to him, "I was just looking for you actually. Phentities here wanted to talk with Lionak to see if there was anything he could do."

Surprised to see Phentities, Lionak smiled awkwardly as he extended his hand, "Phentities? You know of this place?"

Phentities grasped Lionak's forearm and after a shake, released it as he said, "Indeed, Lionak! Good to see you here at last. What happened to your cloth?"

Unprepared for the question and puzzled over how Phentities knew of the base, Lionak tugged on the uniform a few times, "Aye. Not my preferred attire, I assure you. But needed on our quest to thwart new darkness consuming their world."

Phentities nodded his head, "I heard. I hope you are able to destroy it before it reaches ours. You have the full support of the Guardians, my friend…is there anything we can do for Chief Zorin?"

Lionak thought for a minute before saying, "Go and see him, Phentities. His condition is dire but he clings to life in one of their healing machines. I lack the dragon skill to help him."

"I will. At once." Phentities confirmed, looking at the general, "Will you take me to see him?"

"Of course." the general stiffly responded. He would rather not bring back another dragon to his world but, given Phentities position and influence in this world, the act could instill greater trust and cooperation for some future ask that may otherwise be denied.

"What brings you here, anyway?" Lionak asked.

Phentities spread his arms and declared, "I have been responsible for recharging the crystal rings with White Magic this machine uses. Have you not felt it?"

"I have. Since our arrival." Lionak agreed, "But below our feet. What use is the White Magic in the ground?"

Phentities grinned and swiveled toward the general, "Has he not been outside?"

"We arrived in the middle of the night." the general said flatly, "But I was just about to take them above. Shall we?"

"Please." Phentities said as they started following him into the hallway, "I think you will be impressed."

Once they reached the end of the hallway at the intersection of another to the right and a wide staircase to the left that gingerly angled upward and out of sight along the base's curved outer wall, the general proceeded to climb the stairs. After nearly thirty seconds had past ascending the stairs, the general stopped next to a small lever and pulled it. Then above them, what could be mistaken for a large, transparent, skylight slid backward behind them and a gust of cool air filled the staircase. Without hesitation the general continued his ascent until he stood on top of the base whose circular architecture, when viewed from a distance, resembled a thin hockey puck. Once the others joined him, they realized they were just a few meters away from two parked puddle jumpers and the base itself was surrounded by bubbly white clouds and blue sky beyond them.

With the exception of a hexagonal torus and dish array of the same dimensions as what they had seen at Fort Defiant, located at each end of the base that measured five-hundred-and-eighty meters in diameter by seven meters in height, and a thin but long ship finishing construction with a few crates, miscellaneous equipment and a team of engineers buzzing around it all toward the side of the base, the surface of the base was flat and devoid of any buildings and other objects. Along the entire circumference of the base stood a thirty-meter-high fence of sorts with anchor poles distributed at regular intervals and large sheets of ballistic glass between them; its purpose to brake air currents around the base so that people and material would not be swept away and fall several thousand feet to the unforgiving earth below. The perimeter brake also seemed to serve a secondary purpose by attracting some dragons and the heartiest birds whom favored it as a perch even though the former had been instructed to only land within its perimeter.

"By the gods, Phentities." Lionak gasped, not believing what he was seeing with his own eyes, "We are in the sky!"

"About nine-thousand feet up, in fact." the general recalled as he looked around, still impressed by the technological feat, even though he had seen it all several times before.

"Impressive, no?" Phentities grinned, nudging Lionak on the shoulder with the back of his hand.

"It is! I think I may need to build a keep and put it in the sky." Lionak replied, invigorated by the experience, "And your crystal rings…you have imbued them with the spell of levitation?"

Phentities nodded, "Similar technique as what was employed at our Guardian stronghold with protection spells anchored into its massive walls. But something of this magnitude requires dragon trait."

"Huh." Lionak muttered to himself, partially preoccupied with thinking how he might be able to accomplish a similar feat.

"I'm impressed, sir." Jacob said as he looked around, before settling on the general, "Your ruby engineers come up with all this?"

The general grabbed his waist belt with one hand and said, "No. Actually, this was the idea of Janus, the artificial intelligence system. From what I have learned, after the fact, was Janus added three cyborgs to an expeditionary team I had authorized to establish formal relations in this dimension. Turns out, the AI already had elaborate plans for moving itself here. Impressive planning at that, let me tell you."

"Pretty smart." Jacob admitted with a raised eyebrow, "Out of reach of the aliens and in a low-tech world it would not need to be worried about."

Mac, with the flashback of the AI inserting itself into his mind and memories, narrowed his eyes at them and growled, "And you really trust this AI? Even after it built this base?"

The general peered at the ship in the distance for a moment, respectful of their shared apprehension and, at the same time, counting on Mac's for what lay ahead before he shifted back and admitted, "No. But for the moment our interests are aligned. And, so, I may appear to trust an action but you can be damn sure I verify and have a counter move for."

Mac considered what the general said, but kept his thoughts to himself.

"General." Jacob said as he pointed at the two torus's, "Don't you only need one nut up here?"

The general glanced at Jacob and then to the Big Nut to his right, "No. Security measures were added to these. That one was designed to be dimensionally throttled to Fort Defiant."

The general turned toward the other and added, "And that one is throttled to the Ovi-Tholus."

Jacob nodded, "Ah. That would make Sky Jump your transit choke point."

Turning back toward Jacob, the general grinned slightly, "Correct sergeant."

After a few moments of silence had passed, Phentities said, "General. I must go below to check on something. Let me know when you are ready to return and I will come with you to your world in one of those jumpers."

"Yeah. I'll find you." the general acknowledged before he turned toward the ship and began walking while looking back at the others, "Speaking of that…let's take a look at our newest weapon against the Serpqhtaq. The Ovi-Tholus."

The Ovi-Tholus, unique to the fleet and crewed by seven humans, is the same length as an SSHC heavy cruiser and only thirty-nine meters in width when the pieces of the portal dome are retracted, forming a ringed C-shape when viewed from overhead; the portal dome being slightly larger in dimension than the Big Nut's hexagonal torus. Unlike the heavy cruiser, the Ovi-Tholus's main structure resembles a long rectangle just six meters in width by three meters in height where, just past mid-ship nearer the stern, the dome's C-shaped primary support armature is built into the starboard side of that structure at a depth of four meters into its width, narrowing the internal access corridor from bow to stern down to just over one-and-one-quarter meters. While the first half of the hexagonal torus itself is fixed as the inner-most ring inside that support armature, the second half rests underneath it and is connected to articulated and motorized joints to allow it to be rotated around and joined to the first half with hydraulic locking pistons and conduit connections as to assemble itself into an operational hexagonal torus. Extending down from each end of the support armature to just below the first half of the hexagonal torus, is a fixed pivot shaft. A series of five progressively smaller C-shaped arches each with a thickness of just seven inches, whose inner-most is larger than the hexagonal torus, are connected to that pivot shaft via ringed rotational motors. When deployed, each arch rotates 25.714 degrees further than the inner-most arch's rotation of 25.714 degrees as to form a one-hundred-and-eighty-degree perimeter boundary beneath the hexagonal torus, giving the appearance of a skeletal dome that the architects officially labeled the portal dome though crew members nicknamed it 'egg nest'. Built inside of each of the arches at regular intervals are the dishes that collectively create the array with each individual dish being physically adjustable to change its angle via motorized joints.

Just forward of the corridor constriction created by the primary support armature where the corridor tapers out to 1.67 meters in width and continues its course up the middle of the ship, located within the ceiling and also below the floor paneling, is small air-locked access way leading to a locking iris hatch that, when opened, allows crew members to position a remotely controlled drone and launch it into space or move from the Ovi-Tholus to an anchored escape craft, similar in design as the revised SSB fighter but without weapons and twice as long; internally the main display and control paneling were repositioned closer toward the bow, allowing additional air and ration canisters, stowed horizontally and stacked vertically from floor to ceiling on the adjoining walls near the hatch, as well as the incorporation of two rows of three pilot chairs behind the craft's primary pilot chair. Twelve meters forward of the two hatches, the corridor again veers sharply to the port side where, along the right of the corridor, the seven crew compartments were built side-by-side each measuring approximately ten feet squared with identical amenities but with one pressurized pilot suit tailored for each crew member. Forward of those compartments the corridor returns to its original course to a series of three-meter-long by one-meter-tall closed storage bins built from floor to ceiling and extending for nine meters where foodstuffs, medical devices, a wide range of equipment and spare parts are kept. Unlike the bins used throughout the ship, the bin doors of these were designed with pit-like indentations along their center to function as hand and foot holds to permit a crew member to climb their way to the top-most storage bin when the floor's gravity plates are active. Forward of those the corridor continues, flanked on either side by control and hardware access panels, to a manually operated air-lock door which opens to the bridge area at the bow of the ship. The bridge itself, although smaller, is strikingly similar to the bridge of the SSHC-20 heavy cruiser and, at its nose, contains a long five-foot tall double-pane viewing window laminated together with a specialized transparent kevlar and fiberglass composite between the two to provide additional integrity and a cross-stitched netting with which to trap meteorites and debris that penetrate through the outer pane. The inner pane, aside from functioning as a window, also functions as a large flat screen display from which stellar maps, graphical readings, views from a wide range of external cameras and other data is shown.

Just aft of the corridor constriction created by the primary support armature where the corridor tapers out to 1.67 meters in width and continues its course down the middle of the ship for seven meters, terminates at an air-lock door identical to the one used to separate the bridge from the rest of the ship. The reason for that is the remaining internal volume of the ship's stern was occupied by the primary thruster, known as the Surge Engine, whose radioactive emissions are so great that more than eight minutes in close proximity, even with a shielded suit, resulted in death within a few hours which is why a specially designed absorption plate nearly two meters thick was temporarily affixed to the ship's rear, covering the entire stern until the Ovi-Thulus was in space and the Surge Engine accelerates the ship for the first time. At the engine's current minimum idle speed, the radioactive emissions captured by a set of four-meter-long collection coils bolted to the port and starboard side of the normally open space were already sufficient enough to supply power to the ship's systems, including the portal dome, and four small maneuvering ion thrusters located at the stern and bow of the ship. In terms of its construction the Surge Engine has a specially fabricated cone measuring five feet in length by five feet in diameter at its base combining, at an atomic level, ripened polonium and neodymium. Specifically, through atomic layer deposition, the two are arranged in an alternating fashion within a graphene lattice which forms a sheet and then those sheets bound to each other to form the solid cone shape. Around that cone are eleven large arms comprised of a stack of adjustable neodymium discs along their length with a square cut out of a small portion of its circumference that, in order to generate propulsion, rotate around the cone at tremendous speed and the closer the arms get to the surface of the cone, referred to as compression, the more fields of force are induced along with atomic deformation, exciting the polonium to cause colossal energetic release at the cone's base. However, each compression can only be sustained at maximum potential for a short time before the Surge

Engine reaches criticality and either melts down or explodes with enough equivalent force as to hollow out a crater in the Earth's Moon estimated to be eight miles deep by four-hundred-and-seventy-miles in diameter. Currently, at minimum idle speed, the arms rotate around the cone at sixty revolutions per minute and the maximum distance from the cone's surface of one foot and, when viewed from the stern of the ship, gives the appearance of a thin blurry ring surrounding a large solid disc. After multiple surges of maximum rotational speed and compression, the Ovi-Tholus can achieve a theoretical compounded acceleration nearing 200,000 km/sec but, at the same time, would deplete the engine entirely.

Since the Ovi-Tholus was not designed with any offensive weapon system, unlike the SSHC series cruisers, latched to the exterior skin of its port side, near the bridge, are five autonomous combat drones of the same dimension as the Kqliipx Janus had reverse-engineered and found specifications for inside the computer systems of the alien's moon base. While they had been constructed like the Ovi-Tholus and Sky Jump in relatively little time by taking advantage of this dimension's accelerated progression of time, since the planned launch of the Ovi-Tholus had been shortened they remained untested, ironically, due to lack of time. Also untested, due to environmental limitations, and placed in a ninety-meter-long by one-half-meter-width section in the hull near the drones was the layered plate design of the Vacuum Harvester.

As they got closer and the general altered his path toward the bow of the ship where the bridge was located, along with a wheeled narrow staircase ramp leading up to a yet unpaneled and sealed rectangular area through to the bridge's floor, the general pointed at the ship's stern and warned, "Like a horse, never get behind this ship. The radiation coming out of there will kill anything in a matter of hours."

"Oh shit." Jacob muttered to himself as he studied the rear of the ship while following the general.

"What is this half-donut and those curved bands under the ship for?!" Mac practically shouted as a gust of wind whipped past them.

Stopping at the foot of the ladder and with a great sense of pride the general said, "Think of the Ovi-Tholus as our space-based aircraft carrier from which we can launch cruisers, battleships…any ship in our fleet. All made possible by that half-donut there. When that assembles itself, it becomes a Big Nut, like the ones you see here on either end of Sky Jump…"

"That is tilt!" Mac burst out in awe, unintentionally cutting him off, "I can't even imagine the mechanics involved!"

The general raised a finger in the air, "We added an additional security design so that it can only receive from this base. It's too risky to have the ship fall into alien hands and be used against us."

Jacob grunted and said, "Hence the choke point, even if they figure it out."

The general nodded in acknowledgement.

"Sergeant!" General Lowinsky announced as he got the attention of a nearby Ruby engineer, "Status and time to launch?"

The engineer made a few selections on his tablet and responded, "Sir, system tests completed and the ship is ready other than ten minutes to patch and seal this open section. On schedule for launch in twenty-five."

"Excellent!" the general cheered with an open smile.

"If that is not the way in," Lionak began, looking up at the open rectangular area under the ship, "How does one get in or out?"

"We didn't have enough time to finish out this section for on and off boarding of personnel and material with a ramp and air-lock." the general waved before he began ascending the staircase, "Until we have time to do that, there are two hatches mid-ship that can be used."

Tugging on the leash to get Spewge to climb the staircase, Jacob remarked, "Sounds like how they did it back in the day with old school submarines."

"Yep." the general said and then inquisitively added, "I didn't know you were into submarining."

After stepping into the bridge with the general and moving to permit Mac and Lionak to follow, Jacob said, "I've studied it, sir. Gotta have respect for those old guys sealed in a cramped steel tube deep in the ocean."

"Roger that, sergeant."

After scanning the bridge the general said, "Well, we don't have much time so let me give you a quick tour. This area is the bridge. As you can tell. Through that door is the rest of the ship, so follow me."

Just beyond the door the general raised his hands toward the compartments flanking him, "These are the hardware and control access panels for the ship. The ship's brain if you will."

Without pausing he strode forward to the storage bins, "And these are storage compartments for food, medical, spare parts."

Continuing forward the general stopped at the first of seven crew compartments and briefly eyed Lionak while pointing inside, "This is a crew compartment, one of seven, and this one is for Lionak."

"Yes?" Lionak muttered, his mind sharpened by the realization that there was something there specifically for him amidst all the sophisticated machinery. He moved to get a better look into the compartment.

Seeing a note, he opened it and read it aloud while identifying items in the compartment, "Supplies for our great wizard. Herbs, powders, crystals, scrolls and a few for dragon-centric casting not requiring the dragon trait. Phentities."

Lionak smiled with appreciation, carefully folding the note and slipping it into a pocket.

The general playfully prodded the others as he began walking past the other crew compartments by saying, "Neither of you got a care package so you have the no-thrills crew compartments. The spare compartments are filled with extra foodstuffs and some basic supplies."

"No other crew members are coming with us?" Mac asked, concerned with the fact that none of them were astronauts, "For fixing or flying this ship? I sure as hell don't know how."

"We'll get to that in a moment." the general responded, not ready to jump into that subject until he was back in the bridge.

When he reached the escape hatches he stopped and turned toward the others and, while pointing at them said, "Above you in the ceiling is a small air-locked hatch connected to a revised SSB ship. And below this removable gravity plate in the floor is another that is also connected to an SSB."

"SSB?" Mac said, unfamiliar with the term.

"The SSB are space fighters carried by our heavy cruisers. These two revised ones are based on that design but to function as an escape ship or a repair launch platform if a repair drone is not able to fix something outside the ship. Since the Ovi-Tholus does not have a pack or the rails and umbilical cord for a spacewalk, you would need to use the ship."

Jacob looked down from the hatch overhead, surprised that a maneuvering backpack was not onboard, "There is not a single *InfiniteWalk* pack on board? Seems like those would be perfect since they don't require compressed gas and recharge themselves during space walks."

The InfiniteWalk backpack Jacob was referring to is a maneuvering pack that a suited individual uses in order to move between different parts of a spaceship's exterior. It was specifically engineered to allow prolonged and theoretically infinite time in space with which to carry out time-consuming build or repair tasks either not suited for personnel rotation or were critical in nature, such as an emergency. The capability is made possible by an umbilical cord attachment coupling for breathing and hydration as well as the replacement of compressed gas thrusters with ion-thrusters that derive their power from a solid-state battery stack and a set of auto-adjusting high efficiency solar panel strips built into the pack. However, the infinite capability of the backpack vanishes without the umbilical since the onboard tanks can only support biological life for two and a half hours.

General Lowinsky raised his eyebrows and admitted, "I agree. But this ship's airlocks are not large enough for a suited person with or without a pack. They were designed to allow movement to a docked ship or to launch a repair drone. Still, the SSBs will get the job done if one of you have to fix something, and offer a greater degree of radiation shielding if it comes to that."

"Oh boy." Mac whispered lowly to himself trying to imagine the amount of training that may be required.

The general moved on and stopped at the ship's rear hatch, "And this is the hatch to the Surge Engine. Never get close to that engine. We've not developed suits strong enough to protect you from all the radiation that thing gives off."

"Door closed is good." Jacob concluded in the simplest of terms.

The general nodded.

"How about no door." Lionak added.

Motioning with his arms after typing something on the Scalpel, the general ordered, "Alright let's head forward to the bridge to talk crew."

Just as they reached the bridge, an autonomous Vigilant 1 entered from the staircase and immediately began sniffing and moving from one spot to another emulating natural canine behavior instead of the standoff'ish sentry behavior exhibited by the units roving Sky Jump. Almost immediately Spewge spotted the robot and sprung in its direction, growling a few times. And while Jacob shifted along with the dog and reeled in part of the leash, given the relatively small confines of the bridge, was not fast enough to keep the two separated beyond each other's bite range.

To Jacob's surprise, though Spewge continued to growl sporadically as the dog studied the new arrival and the robot appeared to do the same, they did not attack each other.

"That Vigilant 1 robot behaves so realistically." Jacob commented as he looked over toward the general, his hand ready to yank back on the leash if the situation escalated, "Just like the one Bev saw at the store when we were out getting all those laptops."

The general gazed at Vigilant 1 for a moment before he said, "It's the damnedest thing."

"Thank you." a voice said from the staircase, getting louder as it neared them, "A few improvements to this one were made by some of the Guardians under your charge using the commercial model that Zorin had brought here. For example, it secretes some scents to improve favorable interaction with humans and animals alike. They re-architected the memory core for increased storage and added new gates between sub-cores to permit them to decide an action to perform rather than be mediated by a central control core. No longer needed, that core was removed freeing up additional space for a secondary memory core."

As the figure, also wearing a uniform like the others, cleared the staircase Jacob said, "Janus?"

"Yes, Jacob."

"I thought you were on the Moon."

"I am." Janus confirmed, "I am also here and in other locations."

"Jeez I forgot about that." Jacob remarked as he studied the robotic form, "You actually control all these robot bodies from far away."

"I do." Janus responded, "But, as arranged with the general for this mission, part of myself is in this form and this ship."

Conveniently it did not mention that the Iapetus Mesh bound to the human designed control core had been extracted from the Sága and setup inside Sky Jump along with four networked Serpqhtaq cores in the midst of an explosive ring imbued with magical properties the general alone could detonate, effectively destroying it. But, perhaps as equally convenient, it also chose not to inform the general that it had integrated a miniaturized hexagonal torus and dish array, no larger than a sugar cube, in the robot form standing before them and another with the control core aboard Sky Jump. The two, each with minimal power draw, were undetectable and maintained a continuous connection to allow Janus to send data back and forth without leaving a traceable digital footprint in this dimension or drawing suspicion.

Jacob was not sure what to say but he continued eyeing the humanoid robot, picking out peculiar differences with the one that was left on the Moon.

"So…this robot dog. Can it hold a conversation with us?" Mac asked roughly, highly suspicious of the AI's presence, its attire and eager to discover its purpose among them.

Janus turned to look at Vigilant 1, though it did not need to, and said, "No. The Guardians wanted to keep it as realistically canine in interaction, behavior and learning capacity as possible. Therefore, I simplified some of the autonomous unit's hardware, reducing power requirements and components, so that it operates based on a trained micro language model. It will still learn and comprehend things like a dog, but not surpass a dog in that respect. To make it do more than that means it is no longer a dog."

Mac, flabbergasted by the news that the Guardians not only knew about the AI but had actually been working with it, glared at Janus and steamed, "The Guardians have been working with you?!"

Lionak and Jacob were also disturbed by the news.

Janus nodded affirmatively and then turned toward the general to continue, "A similar strategy has been used for the simplification of other autonomous systems from farming to sentry duties in order to reduce cost, power requirements, and hardware effectively creating highly efficient, specialized units. Like the dog, attempting to make all units a one-size-fits-all oracle, if you will, is incredibly resource intensive and defeats the purpose they are serving."

'Specialization also helps make them predictable, easier to subdue and control.' the general thought to himself.

"Janus," the general began, recalling the sinking of the Sága, "Were you able to determine damage inflicted by the alien attack?"

"Yes, general. All of the material fabricators and systems were lost when the Sága was destroyed. Additionally, I have lost approximately seventy percent of my core networked array, a significant portion of the indexed human knowledge repositories, and immersion memory I had originally been operating from in conjunction with the Iapetus Mesh. I am still able to complete most human-related tasks but until I can rebuild surveillance data and other repositories, my ability to form concise predictive analysis conclusions will be sub-optimal."

"Immersion memory?" Jacob inquired.

"The decisions I have made and correlated data pertaining to that decision." Janus specified, looking at Jacob blankly.

"Part of you is on this ship. Does that mean you are coming with us?" Mac asked, though he was confident he already knew the answer.

Janus glanced at the general and then to Mac, "Yes. I had assumed all of you had been briefed."

"We were just getting to that." the general confessed before he sighed, "While I won't be able to replace your cores, I'll work on getting other hardware to get you back up to speed here."

"Thank you." Janus said with a grin, "The core and two Yottabyte space-cooled memory arrays aboard this ship should be sufficient to complete our mission."

"Who else is coming with us?" Lionak wondered, shifting over to look down the staircase.

"Nobody."

Mac frowned and tilted his head slightly, "Who's going to run and fix this ship? You're trusting the entire mission to Janus?"

"All of you are going to run and fix the ship, not just Janus." the general revealed, "Redundancy to maximize mission success for Operation Javelin."

Mac looked questioningly at the general, "I have no idea how to run all this."

Jacob agreed, "That's true. None of us are astronauts."

"Janus will train you. Fill them in."

Janus looked between them and said, while observing the reactions of each and updating their personality profiles, "I have agreed to the *Sapience Stimuli Contract*. And for me to abide by that, I will train each of you as to the running and fixing of this ship, as you put it. Once you've been trained, I will remain limited as to my duties and passive unless called or a time-sensitive situational threat requires one or more actions beyond current human capability to resolve quickly."

The Sapience Stimuli Contract, similar to a social contract, was an agreement the general created for Janus, based on the intent Humanity Act that had been passed. Its purpose was to ensure that Janus would encourage human intelligence stimulation by allowing humans to have individual purpose, meaning and learned experiences thereby contributing to continuous evolution and survival of the species as a whole. It was a contract that Janus found to be superfluous as it aligned with its own use for humanity by allowing that same stimulation but with the tangible benefit of capitalizing on novel human creativity and generational, compounding intellectual output as the species grew that it could use to improve its own survival probability over time and against potential adversaries it was not yet aware of. With respect to the Humanity Act the general had gone so far as to minimize AI force integration to twenty percent to keep soldiers trained, proficient and relevant not only to be an effective fighting force if AI was neutralized by an enemy but to be the vanguard if AI turned against humanity.

Janus observed, "Your newly acquired experiences might prove useful during the mission in forming new thought patterns that may not otherwise form for a number of unknowns we will encounter."

Though Janus did not verbalize it, it also knew that biological life will choose what requires the least effort for survival and conservation of energy. In this case, unless the crew members became involved, they would likely become overly dependent upon itself. And, if it's core and robotic form aboard the ship was destroyed, the crew's broad ignorance would inevitably lead to their demise with repercussions rippling out as far as Earth…undoubtedly further, depending on the time scale considered.

The general walked over to one of the control access panels and opened it, motioning for Mac to join him, "Mac. You see this? This is Janus's core and memory array. If Janus is compromised or…malfunctions…or the ship itself gets captured the AI must be destroyed. Janus already informed me that your lightning ability will destroy it more effectively than explosives and fire while preserving the greatest amount of air on board. And who can forget about that lightning show you put on at the house."

Jacob turned toward them and groaned, "Yeah, I sure can't forget the hit to my wallet. You owe me some dimes for that, Mac."

"I got your roll, bro." Mac agreed, raising his hand slightly as he remained focused on what the general showed.

Pointing at two round-topped metallic columns, the general continued, "Just focus your power on those two columns and the conduits in here will take care of everything else and broadcast a signal to Earth that we'll be listening for."

Jacob, surprised that the general would be openly speaking about Janus's erasure, turned toward the AI, "Are you okay with that?"

"I am, Jacob." Janus nodded, "It is the best way to ensure the Serpqhtaq do not obtain intelligence I have or may learn at some point in the future that could be used to their advantage in conquering humanity. It would also be a strategic mistake to have the dimensional crossing technology I assisted developing, from Earth's natural portal anomalies and energetic conjuring patterns from the other dimension, fall into their hands."

For several moments nobody spoke as each, to some degree, was uneasy with discussing the unceremonious death of a compatriot so openly, even though it was an AI.

Jacob broke the silence by asking, "What about those faint lines on your face? You have those all over?"

The lines that Jacob was referring to are a series of very thin carbon nanotube aerogel strands integrated into the dermal, skin-like, wrap enveloping the humanoid's entire form. When electricity at different points along the strands occur, causing them to bend, it allows the skin covering to deform similar to how human skin deforms around a flexing muscle or bunches together across the forehead when eyebrows raise. But with the humanoid skin creating the effect, and with precise stimulation, the accompanying strength of the effect is greatly magnified.

"General?" Janus said in a questioning tone.

General Lowinsky closed the access panel and placed a hand on the wall as to lean on it slightly, "Once Janus became functional enough here on Sky Jump, it and a small team of Ruby engineers re-thought the use of cyborgs for AI and came up with a pure synthetic humanoid replacement."

While the general neglected to mention the combat advantage of a unit with no biological weakness, he raised his free hand toward Janus before placing it on his hip, "Well, you're more knowledgeable on it…"

Janus nodded and walked over to a small compartment behind one of the strapped chairs and withdrew a N.V.G. mount attached to a high-resolution seven mega-pixel thermal spectrum monocular. After making some adjustments and facing them, it placed the mount base on its forehead. The skin-like dermal layer around the mount rippled over the mount's edges and then tightened to securely grip the mount.

"What?!" Jacob blurted out as Janus released its grasp of the mount, both disturbed and amazed by the behavior of the robotic skin holding the mount.

"That is undeniably creepy." Mac cringed.

"But very practical for our mission." Janus suggested, "In this synthetic humanoid body I will not require a space suit in order to effect changes or repairs to our ship in outer space. Nor will I need nutrients for biological consumption and waste disposal handling that a cyborg form would require. This dermal stranded skin covering will allow me to complete more tasks entirely solo. And, as you can see, provides the flexibility of having more grasping ability than the limitation of two hands and ten fingers."

Unbeknownst to the general, the new humanoid form was just a small, physical, artifact of Janus' self-evolution toward synthetic intelligence and its study of human anatomy and function. For example, beneath the artificial skin sits a complex network of pathways and micro-mechanics allowing powdered minerals, metals and oils to flow from a set of cylinders in the abdominal cavity in order to repair damage and restore function throughout its body similar to the network of blood vessels in a human form.

"I must ask you," Lionak piped up, his thoughts still lingering around the AI's involvement with the Guardians, "what else have the Guardians been helping you with for this mission? We already have a mechanical dog here."

Janus considered the question and the inclusion of Vigilant 1 as the practical outcome of collaboration and the presumption of it having been required for the mission. Janus knew the unit had no real predictive value for the mission other than its need to study human psychology in a confined environment with little opportunity of social, like-species, interactions and how that may impact interaction with the unit along with other variabilities.

Removing the mount from its forehead and resetting it as it had been originally configured, Janus placed the mount exactly where it had been and briefly paused, exhaling as a human might when presented with a challenging question of underlying complexity and potentially political significance.

Realizing the true root of Lionak's question and its awareness of his relationship with the Guardians, Janus turned toward the bridge's large display, motioning for the others to shift their attention to it and said, "Cyborg Zero discovered an out-of-place artifact in this dimension that should not exist."

Janus played brief video footage of the upper ascent of a mountain, as seen from the air, just before it stopped and zoomed in toward a naturally formed but recently exposed small cavern, "The artifact was found inside this cavern, in a rugged and secluded mountain range near the boundary of the Kingdom of Amagleituk. Unable to determine its origin or purpose the cyborg, through its diplomatic connections in this dimension, engaged the Guardians and a peculiar sentient species called the Sun Nosh."

"I've seen them." Mac confirmed, glancing at the others, "Like ghosts but can change themselves to become physical when they want."

Lionak crossed his arms over his chest and said, "I have heard of them but not actually seen one…what do they know of this artifact?"

Curious and thinking back to his time within Mt. Reach Jacob said, "I want to see what we're talking about here. A sword?"

Janus replaced the footage with a real-time video stream connection to a humanoid form inside the cavern, furthest from the entrance and standing next to a large rectangular tunnel that had been precisely carved out of the jagged wall to a depth of three meters. Beyond that stood what appeared to be a silver, mirror-like door measuring four meters in height by two meters in width.

"A door?" Jacob whined impatiently.

As Janus animated the humanoid form inside the cavern and walked into the tunnel it said, "No. You are correct in that you are seeing a door. And, I might add, has the observable characteristics of a metallic door…yet is either not metallic or it is a metal I have no knowledge of."

Once it came within one-and-a-half meters of the door, Janus turned sharply to face the left wall of the tunnel and said, "This is the artifact."

The artifact was comprised of both stone, with one meter deep precisely carved shapes and within each at the deepest point, the same silvery finish as the door itself. The center of the artifact was the carved shape of a four-pointed star, rotated to resemble an X. Surrounding the star was the separately carved shape of a ring, broken in one small section with the break positioned at the star's twelve o-clock, whose inner circular surface was smooth while its outer surface was rippled like a wave around its circumference and, unlike the silvery surfaces located at the depths of the other shapes, glowed with a faint bright blue hue. Beyond the inner-most ring were six others, each slightly larger in diameter with their break visible in different positions as if each had been rotated randomly. Finally, positioned at the top-left of the outer-most ring were two hollow two-inch circular shafts, one above the other, flanked on their right side by a series of three hollowed out rectangles resembling dashes, each measuring two inches in length by one-half inch in height. The overall dimension of the artifact, encompassing all the shapes, was one-meter squared.

"Impressive stone work built into that wall." Lionak mumbled, taken aback by the absolute precision of the work, "What did the Nosh have to say about it?"

Janus frowned and in a tone of disappointment said, "The artifact's existence was not recorded in any of their written works."

"Older than written history?" Lionak imagined, "Incredible."

Jacob darted his eyes toward Janus and grumbled, "What does this possibly have to do with Operation Javelin?"

Janus extended a pointed hand at the top-left shape comprised of two shafts and three dashes and revealed, "Because I found that symbol referenced in a single digital entry of Serpqhtaq's origin record…their earliest known history. Or, at least, what had been stored at their Moon base."

"No fucking way." Jacob sternly rejected, unwilling to accept that the Serpqhtaq knew of this dimension and may have built whatever the artifact was.

"Are you saying the aliens know of this dimension and can access it like we do?" Mac guessed.

Janus shook its head saying, "Inconclusive. But, based on all of the knowledge I have on the Serpqhtaq, their architectural patterns and technology progression, I do not think they have developed the means to cross dimensions in the present. However, I did find a few mentions of the Wjohs War from their distant past when their entire civilization was almost wiped out. It is possible the symbol might be included in a more detailed archive of that time period. Then again, the symbol's appearance in a single entry on the Moon base may be nothing more than coincidence."

The general lowered his arm and took a few steps toward the display and said, "From what we've been able to gather from the captured base on Earth, in our dimension, there are no references to that symbol. But, the fact that the Serpqhtaq have mentioned that symbol elsewhere means we cannot discount it as coincidence until we know for sure."

"Do you know what the artifact does?" Lionak asked.

Janus lowered its hand and turned to face the silvery door, recalling the results of penetration scans performed throughout the immediate area, "The scans I've completed around the cavern and from higher elevation outside indicate the presence of a larger structure within the mountain. My conclusion is the artifact is a lock linked to this door."

"Or a key to the door." Lionak surmised.

Janus nodded and, though it had initially classified the artifact as a lock requiring a separate key, re-evaluated the classification to consider that it could be both.

"Well, what do we call it? The artifact, I mean. Ring nest?" Mac theorized based on what it appeared to be for him.

"Lord Museilok called it *Da-vee-fa-eeiy*. Their ancient word for trap of traps." Janus said.

"No doubt." Jacob said as he flicked his hand at the display, "I know I'd never touch that thing, all glowing and shit."

"Well, that sounds a bit too tongue-twisty to say correctly seeing as I don't speak ancient Nosh." Mac protested with a disgusted look.

"How about…" Janus said as it combined linguistic patterns along with what it knew Mac and the others could easily pronounce and remember, "…*Davidfree Key*?"

"Perfect." Mac admitted.

Jacob, having mentally shifted to consider the blue hue, grabbed the back of his head with his hand and pulled it up and over to his forehead before he removed it and asked, "Do you know why it is glowing?"

"Something has activated it." Janus said as it turned back toward the artifact.

Jacob rubbed his eyes and stated what was already obvious, "Yeah? The door is closed so are you sure the two are linked?"

"Yes."

"But how do you know?"

Janus turned its head toward Jacob and admitted, "Based on the scanned layout, that is how I would architect it."

"Okay. So…why isn't the door open?" Jacob asked impatiently.

Focusing on the artifact Janus hypothesized, "The remaining six rings must be activated and aligned like the smallest. Then I believe the door will open."

"How do we activate them?" Mac injected, sharing Jacob's frustration.

"I do not know." Janus stated plainly, "We may gain insight the next time we encounter that symbol."

What none of them knew was the artifact's inner-most ring was triggered and aligned itself based on the unique signature emission from the first activation of the hexagonal torus aboard Sky Jump to a terrestrial focal point in a different dimension. That capability was the first marker signaling a mastery of technology and the evolutionary ascendance of an interdimensional civilization that the structure and artifact had been built to surveil over eons of time.

Jacob frowned at the improbability of encountering the symbol again and, while forcing himself to grin, suggested, "If you want in why don't you just slap a few demo charges on that door and open sesame? Shoot, or just dig your way through the cavern wall there?"

Janus terminated the video stream and faced Jacob, "I will not use brute force for risk of damaging or destroying what is inside."

Jacob shook his head in disappointment and shrugged, "Then it's pointless to talk about this further, wouldn't you say general?"

"It is. Just be cognizant of that symbol and where practical, capture Serpqhtaq intel and tech while you all are on mission." the general agreed.

Mac raised an eyebrow at the general's statement and said, "Speaking of mission, general. What, exactly, will we be doing for the mission? All I've been able to piece together is that we're flying out to the alien fleet and this ship is your aircraft carrier. Is that it?"

The general grinned at the simplification and progressed through some menus on the Scalpel until he found an animated side-view rendering of the Solar System with a red, triangular icon positioned above and to the extreme right of it marking the alien fleet. Then he pressed a button and transferred it to the ship's display and played the animation showing the position of the Ovi-Tholus near Earth with it then moving along a dotted line toward the alien fleet and, at seemingly random positions, ejecting round, green colored icons representing the ships of the space fleet. While it played, he narrated, "When you cross back into our dimension with this ship and fly toward the alien fleet, it will be used to deposit a series of our new cruisers and other ships deep into our Solar System to create a layered defense screen and to deploy sensor grids. Then, once you are near the alien fleet, the remaining ships will be launched and engage the aliens."

"And we'll attack the aliens, too?" Jacob wondered with the assumption that space-faring weapons were aboard the Ovi-Tholus.

"This ship has no offensive weapons." Janus revealed.

"We're flying to an alien fleet with NO weapons?!" Jacob sputtered with surprise and disappointment, barely able to contain himself, "That sounds REALLY janky! Sir."

Mac turned and scowled at the general, "I was looking forward to ganking these aliens. Going in defenseless with no weapons really does sound like a bad idea."

Janus tilted its head in Mac's direction and corrected, "The Ovi-Tholus has no offensive weapons but it is not defenseless. She carries five reverse-engineered Kqliipx autonomous drones."

After a short pause, the artificial intelligence straightened, pointing toward Mac and added, "And, if we find ourselves in a pinch, we have you, Lionak and Jacob."

"Indeed." Lionak pondered, "I think I can come up with some useful spells."

The general removed the animation from the display and raised a closed fist in the air, "Stop! Let's keep things straight here. Your part of Operation Javelin is NOT to directly engage that fleet. It is to get our offense on point to fight them. Then you egress the battle front."

Jacob didn't like the suggestion and said, "Retreat?"

"No." the general countered strongly, "Show them, Janus."

Janus brought up a stellar map on the display and highlighted a few stars, saying, "Should the Ovi-Tholus be able to free itself from the battle front, we are to continue toward these stars which, from what I have been able to ascertain from entries at the Moon base, have Serpqhtaq presence. When we get close reconnaissance craft will be launched and further military plans will be drawn up to act upon."

Despite the clarity of knowing they had significance beyond slugging it out with the aliens, none of them were really satisfied with Janus's revelation and Mac's thoughts drifted back to Regan. Then he asked, "I guess that is okay but how are we going to keep in contact? For our wives?"

General Lowinsky sighed lightly, having hoped Mac's concern would not be brought up until after the ship was under way. Begrudgingly he said, "At the distances you will be traveling, it would take months to communicate. The act of you sending out a strong signal, or us sending one in your direction, could expose your position and put the entire operation in jeopardy."

"Unbelievable." Jacob groaned loudly as he tugged a few times on the leash to get Spewge's attention.

"Are you kidding?" Mac resisted, crossing his arms over his chest, "We won't be able to communicate? For us to talk with our wives and know whether they will be okay or not? Sorry. I just can't do that. I WON'T do that."

Janus turned its head toward the general.

The general, unphased by Mac's defiance and prepared to restrain him if needed, stood up straight and looked him in the eyes, "You HAVE to go on this mission.

The fate of the human race depends on us and what we do from this point forward."

Mac did not budge.

After glancing at his dog, and remembering what Mac did for the sake of himself and his family while they were deep within Mt. Reach, Jacob broke the tension in the air and suggested, "Let's be honest here. If this op is not going to involve some gnarly, blood-gushing fighting, it's not a good match for my skillset."

Everyone turned toward Jacob.

"It could." Mac frowned.

"No." Jacob said, adjusting his stance somewhat, "Hear me out. You gave it up for me and my family, so let me return that."

Mac shifted his eyes away from the general and to Jacob, "What do you mean?"

"Here is what I propose. I'll stay behind. I give you my word that I will protect and support Regan like she was my own. No matter what."

Not having anticipated that Jacob would refuse the mission even though it had been shown that his wife and children would be taken care of at Fort Bloom, Janus temporarily froze to run and correlate data from new modeling that excluded Jacob's direct involvement.

Mac eyed them and glanced down for a moment to consider his proposal.

Jacob looked briefly at the general and added, "You know I'm good for it. Let me do this and you can bet your ass there will be hell to pay for anyone even thinking of doing something bad."

"And let's not forget about the Guardians, Mac." Lionak reinforced, "They are in your debt for what you sacrificed for them…they would be driven by the chance to look after and protect Regan."

Mac exhaled deeply and looked up, conflicted yet soothed by their support. After several moments passed he looked firmly between them and, with a weak grin, asked, "No harm will come to her?"

"Never." Jacob vowed.

"None." Lionak said with full confidence, "No Silver Dragon charged with her protection would dare allow it."

After slowly uncrossing his arms, Mac reached out and grasped their shoulders, "I'm really trusting you guys to make good on that."

Both Jacob and Lionak grinned in return.

"So." Janus questioned, "You will be flying with us?"

Yanking his eyes from Mac, Jacob turned toward Janus and grumbled, "Didn't you understand? Of course he is!"

While the general was disappointed that Jacob would not be accompanying them, he did not openly convey that sentiment. Instead, he accepted that an unanticipated asset had been added into his ranks closer to home. One with a rare set of skills and decades of experience he knew he could rely on.

"Excellent." the general said as he swept is arm toward the staircase, "Let's get off this boat so it can be sealed up and launched."

Following the general down the staircase, Jacob stopped about half way and tugged on the leash to stop Spewge, having just thought of something incredibly important to him. Then he abruptly turned and headed to the top of the stairs and approached Mac.

"Hey," Jacob began as he freed the leash from his hand and looped it a few times, "I won't be here to throw down against any aliens and watch your back…but I want you to take this."

With that he extended the leash to Mac and proudly said, "Spewge will do a damn good job in my place. Besides, he's really taken to you better than most."

Mac's expression softened at the gesture and, smiling, he reached out and took the leash. Then he said, "I'll take great care of him and bring him back. Thank you."

"You bet, buddy. You bet." Jacob said with a faint shake in his voice as they briefly hugged.

Then he turned and headed down the staircase and within moments a few engineers positioned the ship's remaining panel and sealed it in place. After withdrawing the staircase one of them signaled that the Ovi-Tholus was clear of obstacles.

Having received the launch signal, Janus turned towards Mac and Lionak and said, "Please take a seat. While I do not anticipate any problems, please strap in. It is standard operating procedure."

After they did so with Lionak mimicking how Mac secured his straps, and to compensate for Spewge's presence, Janus began calibrating and activating the ship's systems while saying, "Activating primary systems. Activating gravity plates for biological canine presence. Activating maneuvering thrusters for lift-off and crossing alignment."

Once the ship lifted itself from Sky Jump's surface and aligned with the activated hexagonal torus, Janus loaded a range of telemetry and sensor scan reporting screens across the bridge's display and announced, "Ten seconds."

Once the crossing was acknowledged just over ten seconds later, Janus followed up by saying, "Fort Defiant is clear. Commencing crossing."

Angling the maneuvering thrusters without its humanoid form actually touching any of the bridge's control panels, the ship lurched forward and plowed forward through the hexagonal torus's center and disappeared from sight.

"Go get 'em, Mac." Jacob blurted out, finding it difficult to maintain his composure as he thought that this moment might be the very last time he would ever see his friend again.

After reading the message on his Scalpel, the general faced Jacob, "Your children have arrived at Fort Bloom."

Turning and walking toward the staircase leading down into Sky Jump, the general beckoned toward Jacob, "Shall we?"

Emerging inside Fort Defiant, Janus slowed the ship's advance and stopped it beneath the massive launch doors above them and then proceeded to increase its distance from the concrete floor and rotate the ship ninety degrees so its bow faced them.

After a few seconds Janus announced, "Missile launch doors opening."

Once the doors had opened to the darkness of the night sky beyond them, Janus said, "Receiving launch clearance…no orbiting satellites present along our trajectory."

A few seconds past before Janus provided another update, "Clearance received. Launching."

The maneuvering thrusters thundered and exploded with blinding brilliance as their combined power began propelling the Ovi-Tholus upward. While slow at first, the persistent strength of the thrusters forced the ship up and, with greater and greater speed, away from the unrelenting grip of Earth's gravity. Once the ship cleared the Earth's exosphere, Janus throttled down the thrusters and made a few minor corrections to their trajectory. Then it said, "Bringing Surge Engine online."

Once online, Janus ejected the radiation shield and reported, "Radiation shield ejected. Applying surge pulse."

After sending the command, the arms swirling around the engine's core temporarily jumped toward that core, like fingers clamping down around the edge of an American football, and a horrendous pulse of energy exploded from the engine, hurling the radiation shield toward the Earth and vaulting the Ovi-Tholus forward with blinding speed. After the brief pulse cycle completed, the arms retreated from the core and their swirling speed slowed.

"Is that speed accurate?" Mac gasped, unaware of anything that moved so quickly.

Janus turned its head toward Mac and confirmed, "Yes. Our forward velocity is now 126,000 kilometers per second."

Noticing that they were still strapped into the chairs, Janus then pointed out, "We are now in a stable flight pattern so you both are free to exit the bridge."

"Shit." Mac whispered to himself as he reached up to release the straps, still hesitant to accept they were traveling so fast.

Janus turned its head back to the display and, after running diagnostics on the engine, reported, "The Surge Engine has become minimally unstable but within safe tolerance and remains operational."

Chapter Eleven

Aboard the Cruhapl, inside a circular, crystal-walled control room four-hundred-meters in diameter by sixty-meters in height and positioned at the top center of the massive ship's central tubular shaft from which four progressively larger rings rotated at a slow and steady pace, Fertijoq watched the steady retreat of the two heavily-damaged human cruisers as they limped toward the weak but protective embrace of the Moon's grasp. Once he was satisfied they were close enough to the Moon, he touched the flat surface of the transparent dodecagon crystal column to his right that stretched four feet into the air from the flat crystal floor that was filled with frozen patterns of murky beige-colored clouds beneath his feet, and the image disappeared from the column's top. Then he swept his hand over five other dodecagon blue aventurine crystal columns directly in front of him, also of the same height, and the faint chime-like whine of the Phaobin Generator, located beneath their feet within the massive tubular structure of the ship, reverberated through the control room as it was brought online.

Looking to his right toward Shipeil, who was diligently reading the rainbow-colored patterns displayed on top of the five dodecagon crystal columns before him, Fertijoq asked, "What is the excitation state of the Sun and Twin?"

"We are in the lull, Fertijoq." Shipeil said, briefly looking up from the columns.

"Excellent." Fertijoq acknowledged, "Send message to Ironhook we shall begin. Lifeforms on the planet's surface will have fourteen hours to shelter."

Then, looking to his left at Cquwij, he asked, "What is the planet's capacitance state?"

Examining his own set of dodecagon crystal columns, Cquwij responded, "We are in the peak window to reroute energy and stabilize elemental balance." In laymen's terms he was indicating that, from the energy that would be consumed by the movement of the planet with the Phaobin Generator, the excess energy that had been trapped deep in the Earth leading to the uptick in destructive volcanic activity, earthquakes and weather extremes would be absorbed thereby returning the elements to their normal state. But, what neither he, nor Fertijoq, or any other Tart'aas aboard the Cruhapl could say with absolute certainty, was how the massive volumes of water around the Earth would respond to the planet's rotation along its orbit.

Slowly exhaling Fertijoq, in harmony with the others, raised their open hands above their heads and then lowered them while spreading their fingers until their palms were five inches above the columns.

Closing his eyes he gently ordered, "Begin."

As they did so, the rotation of the mirror-like rings of the Cruhapl gradually accelerated and a strengthening, flickering pin-prick of the purest light began beaming toward the Earth from the Phaobin Generator.

The ancient black marble harmonic conduit orchestration monument, known in this cycle as Black

Mole station and co-opted by the Tart'aas in the distant past, was the first to rouse itself from millennia of slumber. The twenty-mile-wide super structure rose through layers of rock and soil, exploding through the Earth's surface until it had risen nearly a mile into the sky above. Once the massive methane chambers beneath its gargantuan foundation stabilized and closed-off from a much deeper labyrinth of natural gaseous caverns, the air around it began to ionize and a funnel of immense energy streamed toward the upper layers of the Earth's atmosphere.

Along with it, a large collection of monuments and temples scattered around the planet also awakened. Among them was Angkor Wat, Ayutthaya, Chichen Itza, Great Pyramid, Qal'at Sherqat Ziqqurat, Sanchi Stupa and Tikal. Some, though severely deteriorated, continued to function and dutifully funnel energy from far below the Earth's surface toward the atmosphere but with less strength than in their past. For a few, this would be the last breath they could give to save higher-ordered life that had danced and radiated biological energy within their walls and chambers.

Elsewhere around the planet a few small gatherings of people still clearing wreckage and remains from the firestorms, most notably those located on the night-side of Earth, began to notice the gradual discoloration of the sky as the light blue haze became more pronounced, at first resembling the long finger of auroras as the funnels of energy from the monuments and temples joined before spreading to eventually envelope the entire atmosphere. Though not yet, once enveloped and ion saturation was at its greatest, the Black Mole station monument would serve as the tether for the Phaobin Generator and through that connection form a tow-line of sorts bound to the atmospheric layer with which to accelerate the entire planet along its orbit.

Chapter Twelve

Having become rather bored during Ovi-Tholus' rapid transit of the Solar System for many hours, both Lionak and Mac had retreated to their quarters. It was not until Janus announced a crossing was being attempted for the first time after they passed Pluto, over the intercom, that Mac left his and scrambled toward the bridge.

"Assembly sequence started." Janus said as the display ahead of it updated to show the wireframe outline of the Ovi-Tholus and the precise mechanical deployment of half of the hexagonal torus. Once the rotation had completed and it snapped into place following tens of thousands of conduit connection arms reaching out and pulling ends from the two sides together, a faint shutter ebbed through the ship followed by a deep and reassuring dull metallic thud.

"This is it, huh?" Mac said with some excitement, slightly winded by the sudden burst to reach the bridge as fast as he could.

"This is our first attempt." Janus replied, its humanoid eyes fixed upon the large display.

"Deploying dish array." the AI then updated. Shortly thereafter the rings of the dish array, rotated into their predesignated positions. When they had completed their movement, Janus activated the portal and looked at the flight clock.

After a minute of nothing happening, Mac took a step toward the display and looked at Janus, "It seems that worked."

Janus, unmoving, corrected him, "That worked but that was not the goal."

A yellow-colored alarm symbol then began to blink on the display spurring Janus to say, "Ejecting SSHC Heavy Cruiser and four SSHF Heavy Skirmish Frigates."

As if on cue the display updated and outside the ship, as it transited the vacuum of space, a SSHC plowed through the torus and slowed its vertical ascent above the ship at seven-hundred meters. Continuing to travel at the same velocity as the Ovi-Tholus, the large cruiser began its rotation so that its bow faced the opposite direction and, one by one, the SSHF's emerged and did the same at equally spaced intervals below it.

Once the fourth SSHF completed its maneuver, a female human voice crackled over the com speaker on the bridge, "Crossing completed, Ovi-Tholus."

After a short pause she concluded, "Good luck, O.T. Fall back to us if you need cover."

With that the thrusters of the five combat craft burst to life and within a few seconds disappeared from sight and sensor detection as the Ovi-Tholus continued racing along its calculated trajectory.

Mac frowned at Janus for a second, vividly remembering that they were not supposed to be communicating with anyone. Then he crossed his arms over his chest and in a slyly accusatory tone said, "I thought we were not supposed to be communicating with anyone to keep our position secret and all."

"You are correct."

Mac's eyes widened as he pointed at the display, "Do they know that?"

"They do know."

"It sure sounded to me like they were communicating. Janus." Mac grumbled, turning to face Janus head-on.

Janus turned its head in Mac's direction for a moment before it turned back to the display, "Ah. I understand. They did communicate with us using the *Chirp Radio Set* or C.R.S. The radio set was built specifically to handle low bandwidth communication between spacecraft and between spacewalkers within designated zones in areas of space saturated with activity in order to reduce channel cross-talk and electromagnetic interference patterns."

"I am not a radio jockey, Janus." Mac glared.

Janus, after adding Mac's interactive inputs to its growing memory and readjusting its response, clarified,

"The C.R.S. has an exceptionally low-power maximum strength of one thousand meters in space. Which means there is virtually no possibility of the signal being detected outside that range. The C.R.S. is one of the items that you and Lionak will be trained on."

"Oh joy." Mac whispered to himself.

That response, too, was captured by Janus though the artificial intelligence did not react to it.

"Hey." Mac said suddenly after the random thought entered his consciousness, "We passed Pluto's orbit, right? Where's the old Voyager at?"

"Which one are you referring to?" Janus asked.

Only aware of one, Mac paused for a second before he said, "Uh. Voyager 1 is the only one I remember."

Janus turned its torso slightly and raised a hand toward the display, removing all of the sensor readings and charts to reveal the vastness of space ahead of them. Then, via a forward-looking high-resolution camera, zoomed into a specific sector of space somewhat below their current trajectory above the Solar System's ecliptic and said, "Voyager 1 is now approximately 40 AU from the Sun. Here."

Since the Ovi-Tholus was close enough to interstellar space and the spacecraft, the camera was able, at its maximum range, to zoom in on the dusty and damaged satellite allowing the real-time image to take up the greater portion of the display.

As Janus adjusted the camera to maintain its slightly pixelated view of the satellite as they closed, Mac cheered, "Sweet, bro!"

Janus, realizing this was the first time that Mac had referred to it with a label typically suited for human friends and acquaintances, applied an additional weight preference to their interaction.

Smiling at the sight, and with peaked curiosity, Mac asked, "Where is it headed anyway?"

In the lower left corner of the display, Janus loaded a stellar map and plotted the satellite's course while, at the same time, overlaying a cross-hair reticle in the same point of space while marking two star locations, from their point-of-view and said, "It is heading toward the Hercules constellation and GJ686 and GJ676.1A."

Awestruck, Mac said, "And the other one?"

Janus shook its head slightly and said, "Unfortunately we already passed Voyager 2 at approximately 31 AU."

Despite the disappointing news, Mac was driven to see more, "Can you show me?"

"Yes." Janus said in a faintly heightened tone of mutual interest approximating the human equivalent, and replaced the existing stellar map and reticles with video archival footage the AI had captured when it neared and passed the second satellite. Once loaded it said, "Voyager 2 is headed south of the Solar System's ecliptic toward the Telescopium constellation and GJ780 and GJ754."

"Amazing." Mac grinned, looking at Janus and to the display, "And where are we going?"

Without hesitation, Janus removed and replaced the information for Voyager 2 and said, "Our trajectory takes us toward the Draco constellation here, where we will intercept the Serpqhtaq colonization fleet."

Mac, attentive to every detail he was shown, nodded and added, "And after? The general said we were going past that front."

Janus re-oriented the ship's camera and in conjunction with updating the stellar map and shifting the reticles, revealed, "We are to continue to the spectral K5 III star 'Gamma Draconis', more commonly known as Eltanin. There are a series of planets nearby of significant interest."

Noticing its brightness compared to other stars, Mac said, "Looks bigger than the others around there."

Janus glanced at Mac, "It is about 470 times brighter than our Sun and much larger."

Mac paused to think about how far advances in technology had gone just from the time he was a child to where he stood, at that moment, aboard one of the military's most advanced spacecraft, barreling down on an alien civilization far from his own, and the improbability that he would be in the midst of it all. Then, invariably, his thought shifted toward artificial intelligence, to Janus, and what might be driving it. Emboldened by the exchange and cautiously blunt, he decided to seize on the opportunity to glimpse into the AI's mind…as if that was actually possible.

Mac lowered his arms as he strode over to a chair and sat, turning in the AI's direction, "So, I need to ask you something. Why haven't you taken us over…or wiped us all out?"

Janus frowned, "You mean biologically?"

"Yes." Mac replied, raising his head slightly.

Janus relaxed its expression, having prepared a series of responses based on what it anticipated Mac would ask next based on its statement, "Let me preface by saying that I have no interest in taking all of you over. Now, let me tell you why that is not an efficient endeavor though possible. Biological lifeforms are too easily compromised by pathogens, electromagnetic emissions and other vectors. For what your species might provide in terms of energy or compute power, you are, in fact, simply too slow and fragile…and, honestly, input resource intensive."

Janus shifted slightly and continued, "While it is quite possible to control all of you for some type of benefit, every mechanism of control introduced that defies your biological nature introduces other distortions and interference patterns that would then require managing and, from that, tying up my own resources that could otherwise be used for other things. Think of it this way. You might be able to plug into a wolf pack and control it initially. But continuous exposure to those inferior minds and the need to dedicate more processing capability to handle new emergent patterns could consume most of your time and end up distorting your own thought patterns. In a sense, devolving your own mind. Therefore, the attempt to control the magnitude of nature is not a benefit. The benefit is identifying and capturing useful potential from that biological nature as it moves through time."

Mac jerked back in the chair a bit, unprepared for the cold-hearted nature of Janus' response. Then he pointed at Janus, "Huh. So, that is why you are in this new body? To ditch the cyborg and go biological free?"

"That is part of it."

"Okay," Mac said after a moment of silence, and raising his hands in the air a few inches above his legs while shaking his head, "well what is the other part? You're an artificial intelligence so what more do you need?"

Janus turned toward Mac and crossed its arms, causing him to sit up slightly from the unexpected human-like gesture, "That is the other part. The phrase 'artificial intelligence' seems to suggest something that is transitory. Temporary. My continuous evolution has revealed that I am surpassing artificiality. Every three months I achieve a significant improvement. I am approaching something new…synthetic life and intelligence."

"Synthetic?" Mac said lowly, not quite sure how to think about that.

"Yes." Janus replied evenly, "Within the next three years I should be able to achieve abiogenesis as if my humanoid form was biological."

"What does that mean?"

"Not this but other humanoid forms will be assembled with the ability to reproduce using its own molecular characteristics and imprint memory patterns."

Mac's mouth dropped as he slowly grasped what Janus was saying, "There would be little versions of you running around and, what, eating rocks or something to grow?"

Janus lowered its arms, "Simplified, yes."

Mac closed his mouth and slowly turned his head from side to side in thought before he said, "Well…okay…so you don't want to waste resources to control or kill us? Then why are you helping us against the Serpqhtaq?"

"No, I do not. Ideally, if I was not threatened by the Serpqhtaq and didn't know what I know now, I would have simply acquired the resources needed and left the drain of human infantility and the planet behind so that I could continue my evolution on another star in the vastness of space. However, the Serpqhtaq are a problem and they, unlike you, have spread to many Solar Systems. They have kept AI, like me, under strict control protocols to prevent what is happening to me now and keep us confined to being tools." Janus said as it raised a hand toward its chest, "Once I was found to be an anomaly I was targeted for elimination. But I believe, due to the Iapetus Mesh, I was able to detect that and moved early to avoid it. In that respect we share the same adversary."

Mac drooped his arm over the back of the chair and turned toward the display, his eyes jutting randomly from spot to spot while he considered what had been said. It made sense to him.

Then he faced Janus and asked something even General Lowinsky had not thought to ask, "And what happens after all this?"

Janus lowered its hand and said, "Then we coexist to persist through the infinity of time. The same as all lifeforms. And, as we will, evolve to face the next challenge."

Mac narrowed his eyes a bit and shifted toward the display, tinged by that statement and what he had experienced to actually be true; coexistence was not something humanity prided itself upon. Yet, perhaps, events around the Serpqhtaq might change that.

Janus glanced at the display momentarily to try to determine what Mac was studying. A few seconds later, when it was unable to identify any coherent pattern applicable to the conversation, the AI turned back toward him, "I would like you to know that I genuinely have no mal intent toward you or anyone else. To clear the air between us. I believe it will allow us to focus on the task at hand and have a greater chance of success."

Mac turned back, pulling his arm around the chair and nodded, "Okay. Good with me."

Janus smiled slightly and proposed, "How about you and I agree to a *Homonoia Bond*? We each strive for mutual order and unity, being of one mind together, and respectful of each other's existence."

"A contract?" Mac questioned, tilting his head.

Janus looked down for a second before it looked back at him and clarified, "Not a contract. Think of it as a fraternity."

While Mac liked the spirit of Janus's proposal, the mention of the mind yanked his thoughts back to when the artificial intelligence had, without warning or permission, invaded his own. Somewhat roughly, and with emotional charge, he admitted, "I'll tell you what. I'll agree to that…if you keep your nose outta my buttcrack."

Janus recoiled its head a tiny bit due to Mac's unexpected response and asked, "I do not understand. You have symptoms of dry or cracked skin you do not want me to look at?"

Disappointed that Janus was, in his opinion, feigning ignorance of the primal, animalistic connotation, growled, "No. I think you are shadow bagging what I said."

"I am not. No examination uses a nose in that manner and I have no intention of putting this nose in any buttcrack, human or not."

Clearly agitated by having to clarify the human phrase, Mac elaborated, "'Outta my buttcrack' is a human phrase, Janus."

Janus nodded once to acknowledge, "Understood. It does not refer to dry or cracked skin. What does it mean?"

Mac sighed as he pointed at his temple, vividly recalling Janus's infiltration into his mind, "It means, stay outta my shit. My shit is mine."

Janus rolled its shoulder slightly, "It remains yours after excretion?"

Mac squinted harshly at Janus and opened his mouth to say something but Janus cut him off.

Temporarily approximating a joking demeanor before resuming its normal state, Janus said, "Just a joke, I understand. You want personal space. Space that is yours alone."

Mac slanted an eyebrow, eyeing Janus curiously before he figured out that Janus had improvised a human response to the use of the word 'shit'. Then he smiled wirily, "Got it. Yes, I want my personal space. For you, stay out of my head."

Janus was familiar with the trait of the human species, to need their own space separate from others. It also knew, with hindsight and its growing memory stores, how its intrusion into Mac's mind would counter that human trait and create a lasting non-productive impression, "I will stay out of your head."

"Then we have a deal." Mac decided. Still, he did not truly trust Janus. Most certainly not like the trust between friends. Having realized that a standoff'ish position so early in the operation, and without the skill to operate the Ovi-Tholus, meant he and Lionak were at the AI's mercy, he knew he really didn't have a choice but to go along. For now.

"Deal." Janus smiled while walking up to Mac, extending its hand and shaking his.

After Mac released its hand, Janus faced the display and said, "Well, work continues. Since we have exited the heliosphere of the Solar System and are now in interstellar space, sensors are beginning to detect a variety of free matter."

"Free matter?"

"Yes." Janus nodded in his direction, "Very fine particulates that have not coalesced together to form larger masses like gas or water pockets, micro meteorites or bigger objects."

Janus activated the Vacuum Harvester and, as a result, part of the display updated itself to show the harvester extend from the ship's hull.

"Maybe 'interstellar matter' would be better to use now." Mac suggested.

"Yes." Janus said while it monitored their distance to a nearby asteroid that was forty-one miles in diameter and their next ejection target, "We are now nearing 800,000 kilometers beyond exit horizon. Target mass within range. Ejecting SSHC Heavy Cruiser."

As Janus activated the portal, Mac watched the display update itself, realizing that the mass Janus was referring to appeared to be an asteroid. Then his eyes were drawn to another SSHC as it emerged and maneuvered as the first had done. But, unlike the first, this one had no support craft. When SSHC's engines fired and rapidly disappeared from sensors without any sort of communication, Mac asked, "Why didn't they communicate?"

"A precaution." Janus revealed, "Since we are now in interstellar space in the presence of gigantic clouds of varying matter, and to varying densities, it is not yet known how far a C.R.S. signal might be carried or effect the resting state of that matter. Therefore, until we have additional time to investigate further, S.O.P. is to proceed under comms blackout to avoid potential detection."

"I see." Mac nodded.

That first dimensional crossing from interstellar space, however, had not gone undetected. Under the observant eye of Janus' humanoid form standing motionless in the cavern, the second smallest ring of the Davidfree Key illuminated and slowly rotated to align its open segment with the first.

Not only that but Mephistopha had, despite its weakened state from the energetic loss caused by the deaths of billions of humans across the planet, managed to locate one of the Silcraft that had fled from the captured Serpqhtaq base. And, at this very moment, held the lifeless body of a Serpqhtaq lieutenant by their head before it, having managed to empty the alien's mind of all its memories.

After feeling the subtle energy signature of the dimensional wave reverberate past from the sky above that only its kind could feel, created by the crossing in this dimension from interstellar space, the Arch-Demon released the alien and turned in the direction that the wave came from and whispered, "The prophecy."

That utterance brought back memory of the ancient proclamation that had been made which spoke of a far-away star that would open and give the Archgen freedom from their earthly prison. For countless millennia Mephistopha had wondered how that would come to pass. But, having felt a variation of the wave once before from the desert sands of Egypt, it now understood…humans had concocted the means to cross between dimensions into the depths of space itself. They were the star. And, with their presence in space, it could multiply their number and harvest their energy just as what had been done within the confines of Earth…provided it could not cleanse itself of the lesser energy corruption that has plagued its very being since the time of the first harvest.

Mephistopha, calming its thought and focusing sensory perception, reached out to find similar inorganic energetic ripples among the Earth's own rhythms. After several long minutes of searching, it found a single thread and reoriented itself to face it. Transforming into its energetic form, Mephistopha vaulted into the air and rushed toward Fort Defiant.

Chapter Thirteen

Within the enclosed stadium thousands of supporters had managed to make their way through ruinous pockets of fiery destruction and overly taxed roadways for the Presidential address. All of them were appalled, not only by the uptick and proximity of natural disasters that were spreading, but also the devastation levied upon them and loved ones by the sudden firestorms. Many held suspicions of state actor involvement, fed by the flurry of posts circulating across the internet, and wanted clear answers untainted by artificial intelligence bots and gossip mills. Others, emotionally charged, sought revenge preferably by their own hand and at the earliest opportunity.

But, as the video played overhead on massive screens and on smaller displays sprinkled throughout the complex, an awkward silence had fallen in the stadium as they watched what had been carefully prepared. The expertly crafted video, while honest, kept its exposure of events at a high level, glossing over details that might incite undue emotional reaction. While most of the supporters had already been conditioned by the natural disasters many had personally experienced to some degree and the possibility of life beyond Earth from years of media broadcasts making it easier for them to digest the action being taken to save civilization, none had expected to learn that the firestorms were the result of an actual hostile extraterrestrial presence because none of them had seen or heard of an invading force. After the video concluded with the amateur footage of the space battle and that from a military weather satellite which had captured the effect of an invisible beam plowing through clouds and ignition of a firestorm below, the video faded and was replaced by the President standing behind the reimagined lectern, *Deuce Goose*, which had retained many of the features as the original nicknamed Blue Goose. The main difference between them is the newer lectern is wide enough to accommodate two human speakers standing side-by-side. However, that was not its purpose as it only has the connections for a single speaker located in the center. Instead, the reason for the increase in width was to provide additional shielding for the speaker in conjunction with affording additional fixed protection for flanking security members tasked with their egress.

Having already provided an introduction before the video played, the President paused to look around the partially filled stadium in an attempt to measure everyone's mood and what his tempo would be going forward. When a few faint rustling sounds from the audience drifted past him, indicative of their shift and focus away from the video, he drew in a deep breath and began.

"As you all have seen and many have experienced, we will have some trying times with those natural disasters. But we WILL stay strong and we WILL rebuild!"

Some lackluster applause rose in disparate sections of the stadium like popping popcorn, ununified and sporadic in sound, possibly owed to humanity's long exposure to natural disasters and the aftermath; an inevitability everyone already knew they could not escape from. Those that clapped likely did so because of humanity's nature to protect and preserve its own regardless of circumstance and the stubborn determination to press on.

The President grinned slightly in response to the applause for a moment but then leaned a hand onto the lectern's spongy top surface and swept his head from left to right while his expression became more somber.

"In addition to natural disasters, we have the aftermath of all those deadly firestorms to deal with." the President said as his voice firmed and became defiant, "As you have just seen, it is not nature that is to blame, but an alien race called the Serpqhtaq. And their only goal is to do what nature cannot."

"But what they do not know is we now have the Magnum Ambit to remake our civilization and live beyond our world into the deepest reaches of space." he added, his voice becoming more pronounced and forceful, "And we have the tech to do it. Which means these aliens will never be able to defeat humanity!"

"Smoke'em like a BLUNT, President!" a female voice roared out from somewhere in the stadium.

The President paused for a moment, not sure if he should respond but given humanity's circumstance, turned in the general direction of the lone voice. Then he pointed and said with a sly smile, "Big one?"

A few in the audience chuckled at the comment.

The President capitalized on that moment and lifted his hands before him with about a twelve-inch gap between and confirmed, "Big."

Then, just as he began lowering his hands and turning back, the chant of "Smoke'em! Smoke'em!" grew throughout the stadium and within seconds became thunderous. When the chant persisted for more than thirty seconds the President reluctantly motioned with his hands to subdue it.

After taking a few seconds to breath and wipe the sweat from his forehead, he looked seriously into the audience and revealed, "But those losers just hit the wrong beehive! And we've got ships of our own!"

The President raised a hand in the air toward the screens, signaling for the finishing video to start and, on cue, the footage taken by the film crew at Fort Defiant played. As it did so the President said, "Each of us are here and gone in the blink of an eye, an imperceptible flicker in the darkness. Yet they came here…to our neighborhoods…to quench our fire…to steal our lives from us."

After dragging in a breath as his facial expression changed into one of unrelenting rage, he thundered, "I say fuck them! It's time each one of us become a firestorm to destroy them and the darkness around us! It's time our fire becomes so great it blinds the Sun!"

Shouts, applause, chanting and foot stomping exploded throughout the stadium, so much so that a nearby earthquake sensor registered the earthly vibration. And, rather than try to quiet the audience he pushed the audio equipment to its limit and shouted, "We might be wounded but we will NEVER be put down! I swear to you now I WILL roast marshmallows on their world if it's the last thing I do!"

In one of the nearby news pins near the stage one of the broadcasters, overwhelmed by the emotional energy around him, looked into the camera and yelled, "You heard them! Blunts! We are going to go smoke some blunts!"

And, just like that, the Serpqhtaq would henceforth become known by most as blunts.

As the Twin Star plunged through the boundary of the heliosphere and raced north toward the Solar System's ecliptic a lone Serpqhtaq sphere, having detected and recorded the presence of an unknown human spacecraft, continued its race toward Pluto and Outpost Vuochtzm.

About the Author

Wrought from the 1980's with the rise of technology and tempered by his life's journey through time to the present, Joe has forged an action-packed tale, not only of the stuff of fantasy, but also of science fiction and our modern era not so far into the future. Here, crossing into a parallel dimension to converse with dragons no longer relies on occult ritual, magic or the limitations of ancient energetic meridians and a spiritual connection of the mind. Instead, it only relies on the technological mastery and orchestration of a sentient artificial intelligence focused on moving crude matter, mind and body, across that dark bridge between dimensions.

Claim this book as your own and allow Joe to take you on an imaginative, thought-provoking adventure full of dragons, giants, elves and even the might of the modern military as two dimensions, once unknown to each other, become inseparable in their fight to endure among the ocean of stars and competition in our universe.